Hold Tight
Willow Springs Ranch
Book Two

Laura Harner

I0457220

Copyright

Hold Tight is a work of fiction. Names, characters, places, and incidents are the product of the author's imagination or are used fictitiously. Any resemblance to actual persons, living or dead, events, or locales is entirely coincidental.

Dedication

To Cowboys everywhere. It's the spirit that counts.

I always offer a special thanks to D.W.S. Photography, but this time, there are not words enough to express my gratitude to my friend Dan Skinner. The character, the book, the series...they would not exist without his inspiration.

I would also like to offer a special thank you to Tom Webb and Jae Ashley for their many contributions.

Trademarks Acknowledgement:

Table of Contents

Prologue

"What the fuck do you mean he's on the way to the Willow Springs Ranch?" Sheriff Holden Titus shouted into his phone as he hurried into the kitchen.

Ty and Cass stopped their conversation to look at him as he struggled to untangle the Velcro tabs on his Kevlar vest. God this was just another cluster-fuck. Everything had been under control. Then one of his goddamn deputies located the suspect the entire county was looking for and decided to let him go? He shouted directions at the hapless officer who'd drawn the short straw and had been the one to call in the fuck up. Now the suspect appeared to be driving straight here to the ranch, the location of the original cattle killing crime. He hoped to God the man wasn't looking to come after ranch-owner Cassidy Cartwright or his partner Tyler Hardin.

Holden wrapped up his conversation with a few terse orders then turned to face the two men. He apprised them of the situation, noting the way Cass moved closer to Ty while the former Navy SEAL seemed to bow up slightly, as if he was preparing for battle. He knew the man could handle himself, but given his struggle with PTSD, he'd just as soon the two men go somewhere else for a bit. Just in case the fugitive had fighting on his mind.

"I suggest—" His words were lost in a thundering explosion that rocked the kitchen to its foundation, shattering glass and raining hell upon all three of them. He couldn't exactly say his life flashed before his eyes, but the regrets certainly did. In the remaining seconds of his life, Holden Titus saw a perfect vision of the future he would never have.

Chapter One

Holden pulled back on the right wheel and turned his chair in a slow circle as he looked around the room once more. He knew he hadn't forgotten anything, but it was a compulsion with him to leave everything in order.

"You ready, big guy?" Tyler asked from the doorway.

"More than goddamned ready," he said.

"Oh, no, Mr. Ty. You're not allowed to wheel the sheriff out." Annie, the petite Asian nurse who had tried her best to terrorize Holden for the last six weeks brushed the former Navy SEAL out of her way, like he was nothing more than a pesky housefly. "The rules say it must be one of the staff. Let's go Mr. Crabby Pants. Ty, you grab his bag. Did you bring the low car like I told you?"

"No, ma'am. We have to drive the truck to get to Willow Springs Ranch."

"I'm not a damn invalid," he said, automatically picking up the thread of their daily grousing match.

"Oh yeah? I don't see you walking out of here on those two fine legs."

"Bitch."

"Yes. But you're going to miss me."

He would, but he wasn't going to admit it. No one spoke as he endured the indignity of letting Tyler lift him into the cab of the truck. Then Annie climbed onto the running board of the ranch truck, and pecked him on the cheek.

"Just because the rules say we had to use the wheelchair to take you outside, doesn't mean you're supposed to use it all the time. Get up on those legs and make them work. You follow the doctor's orders, and do your damn PT, Titus, or I'll kick your grouchy ass." Without another word, she hopped down, slammed the truck door closed and pushed the chair back through the automated doors on the front of the glass vestibule of the long-term rehabilitation facility. Holden looked out the side window of the truck as they rolled away from the building that had been his home since his release from the hospital six weeks earlier. Now, he technically had no place to call home. He blew out a frustrated breath.

"Look, Ty…you don't really have to do this," he said. He immediately realized the stupidity of the comment. What the fuck else was he supposed to do? His legs didn't yet work right, he couldn't drive, and he had blinding migraine headaches. Cass and Ty had already packed up his second floor apartment and put his belongings in storage. The only place he had to go was the Willow Springs.

"Cass and I wouldn't have it any other way. Cass blames himself, you know. You were at his house, trying to protect us. If you hadn't been there you'd never have been hurt."

Blinking rapidly and swallowing around the frustration, he tried to offer his own reassurance. "I won't stay long, Ty. I just need a couple of weeks to figure out what I'm going to do. The docs don't figure I can go back to..." he trailed off. What the fuck was he going to do now? No job, no home, and responsibilities weighing on him that weren't going to go away.

Ty patted him awkwardly on the arm, but kept his eyes on the road. "Holden, there isn't anybody on the planet that knows exactly how you feel right now, but I expect I'm pretty damned close. You talk when you're ready. We've got a few things planned, including introducing you to Perry, my counselor at the VA. He's really good with PTSD. I mean, I'm not saying you have that or anything," Ty stammered. "We just thought...I mean Cass and I just thought it might be a good idea."

Holden glanced over at the handsome man with the scar marring the right side of his face, from hairline to jaw. Medically discharged midway through his Navy career, no longer able to do the job he thought he'd do his entire life. He remembered that Ty had come to WSR to spend some time with Gibby, his Navy mentor and surrogate father, only to discover the man was dead. Suffering from debilitating PTSD, Ty had been in a bad way, but Cass had taken him in and the two men seemed to fit each other just right.

"Thanks, Ty. I don't know what to feel."

"You feel what you feel. There's no right or wrong. It's going to be weird at the ranch because that's where everything happened."

Thinking about it, he decided he could tell Ty. "I don't remember any of it. They've placed Morgan in as acting sheriff, and he brought me some of the reports. I know you said I was on the phone, but I have no memory of anything after dinner."

The salsa beat of his ring tone interrupted his recollection. He pressed the button on his new phone, courtesy of Cass. "Titus," he answered. After the brief, one-sided conversation, Holden closed his phone.

The road was nothing more than two-lanes stretching endlessly into asphalt ribbons. The waves of heat created ever-elusive puddles of water, mirages that hovered always just in front of the truck but never attainable. A fucking metaphor for his life.

It would be easier to tell Tyler alone, before they arrived at the ranch. "Well, it's official," he said. "The mayor accepted my letter of resignation based on medical disqualification. The city wants to settle on an amount of compensation as soon as possible. They'll have to cover all medical expenses outside the insurance, but that's about it."

"Talk to Cass before you settle anything," Ty said. "Trust me on this, Holden. Now, hang on, it's going to get bumpy," Ty said. They turned onto the rough graded road that wound for twenty-five miles before eventually leading to the Willow Springs Ranch turn off.

Holden blew out a breath and shifted his legs to try and get into a more comfortable position as the truck bounced over the rutted dirt road.

****

Cass stood looking out the window of his study in the long, low adobe main house. He watched his lover lift Holden from the truck and place him in the borrowed wheelchair. The chair moved easily enough over the hard-packed dirt. Holden expertly maneuvered in a circle, then made for the low ramp the hands had added to the front of one of the twin casitas. Over the years, the small adobe houses had served as homes for the ranch cook and the ranch foreman. Currently both were empty and it seemed like a good idea to put Holden in the recently renovated unit. Using crutches and a wheelchair without help in his second floor apartment would have been nearly impossible. Cass had wanted him in the main house, but Ty had been right when he'd said although Holden was injured, he wasn't going to need permanent care. It was important that he kept a sense of independence all the way through his recovery.

Cass wanted to go help Ty, go greet Holden, but his feet might as well have been nailed to the floor. What the fuck do you say to a man whose whole life changed because of you? Oh, he knew in a logical sense it wasn't his fault. The fucking prick, Tony, had tried to kill them all. Still, if Holden had just left after gathering his evidence instead of—

"Well it's just not the way it happened, now is it Cartwright, so get over your damned self," he said aloud.

He moved to his desk and aligned the folders, checked through his list once more, then sat to wait for Tyler and Holden. It wasn't long before the two men emerged and headed to the main house. Tyler was big enough to be a professional running back at just a touch over six feet and weighing in at two hundred and five pounds. Broad and hard in all the right places. Cass had to quickly shift his attention to the other man or risk meeting their guest while sporting wood.

Looking at Holden erased any thoughts of sex from his mind. The man was still good looking, with his chestnut colored skin, powerful arms, and barrel chest. But it hurt to see his big frame trapped in the wheel chair. As the two men approached they chatted easily enough. Ty casually walked alongside Holden's chair, making no effort to help, as the other man powered his chair over the hard-packed earth. The two of them had a lot in common, both former Navy, both injured in explosions, both having to carve out new lives for themselves from the ashes of important jobs. He hoped what he had to offer would be enough. For both of them.

"Welcome, Holden. Good to see you here," Cass said. He felt awkward and foolish. What the fuck was he supposed to say?

"Cass." Holden gave a brisk nod and he wheeled into the study. He used his hands to brake the chair then rotated one wheel until he turned to face the rest of the room. "I appreciate you having me here." Gesturing toward the window, he continued. "You went to a lot of trouble with the ramps. And I sure wasn't expecting one of the casitas. I don't need much more than a room, you know. I'll be out of your hair—"

"Shut up, Holden," Cass said. As soon as the words were out of this mouth a sense of relief flooded through him. He grinned at the shocked expression on Holden's face. Suddenly he felt on steadier ground. This wasn't about his own feelings...he needed to make Holden feel at home.

"The three of us might be new at this friends business, but I think we can manage. You're welcome to stay as long as you want. We've got two vacant casitas right now, and I see no reason at all you shouldn't stay in one of them."

Blowing out a breath, Holden gave a quick nod. "All right. Thanks. I'm not quite sure...things are just..." he trailed off, glancing toward the window.

"Hey, Holden," Ty said, moving to sit on a couch near the wheelchair but not too close. "Don't try to overpower what's happening. You've got some healing to do and a lot to think about, but you also have some time. Okay?"

Holden nodded, looked at Ty, then over at Cass before dropping his gaze to stare at his own legs. "Yeah. Well...we'll see. It's pretty evident my career in law enforcement is over. I'm not sure what the fuck else I'm cut out for."

Cass winced at the bitterness in the tone. Ty looked over and mouthed an order. *"Tell him."*

There was a tightness in his chest as he realized his lover knew more about the changes in Holden's life than anyone because of their shared similar experiences. If he wanted Cass to push at Holden a little right now, then he would.

"Maybe. Do me a favor, Holden...take a look at this." Grabbing the folders from his desk, Cass crossed the room, and held out a folder to Holden. When the other man made no move to take it from him, Cass dropped it onto his lap, then took a seat on the couch next to Ty.

"Look at this record, tell me what you see." He turned his back to Holden and carried on a quiet conversation with Ty. After a long pause he heard the rustle of paper and knew Holden had been unable to resist looking at the contents.

Several minutes later, Holden interrupted. "Okay, I've looked. What do you want to know?"

As Cass turned to face Holden, Ty gave him an encouraging wink. Ty had explained that what he'd mourned most when he was first discharged was the sense of purpose that came with knowing you belonged, that you were a part of something beyond yourself. They'd come up with something that they both hoped would help Holden's internal cop see that he was still necessary. Ty had warned that the first reaction was likely to be anger and rejection. So Cass steeled himself for both.

"Do you think I should hire this man?" Cass asked.

Holden's eyes narrowed, drawing his brows together in a frown line. His dark fingers tapped against the manila folder. "My first instinct is to recommend against it, but if you insisted, then I would recommend checking with the foreman at the last couple of places. I would certainly have to know more. Why? Did he apply here?"

"This was Tony's record. I paid a fortune to a private security firm to acquire all of these records. Of course, it's a damn sight easier to figure out you might have a homicidal maniac on your hands, after the fact."

"Most of the information in this report would be readily accessible with a simple background check and a few calls to previous employers. Whoever you hired to do this shouldn't have needed to charge a fortune," Holden said, obviously interested.

"That's how I figure it, too. The problem is, we don't have access to the data, even in this day of the Internet, unless we pay for the specialized reports. For the smaller ranches that's just too damn much money. And who the hell has time to do the searches and analyze the reports even if we did pay for them?

"I've been talking with some of the owners around the tri-state area. There are hundreds of ranch hands and itinerant workers during different times of the year in this part of Arizona, Nevada, and California. This incident with Tony wasn't the only time one of us has been burned by hiring someone who could have been weeded out with a simple search by someone more experienced than any of us. We know cows. Or lettuce. Or horses. We want to hire you to figure this background shit out for us." Cass was about to go on, even as he saw the heat building in Holden's face.

He held up a hand to try to forestall the coming storm, but the slam of the front door distracted them all for a moment.

"Hope you don't mind I let myself in," a voice called from the front of the house. Cass closed his eyes briefly. *Drew.* Otherwise known as Andrew Van, the local large animal veterinarian could be heard taking off his boots and then moving toward them, a running commentary about his reason for arriving unannounced.

"Hey, Cass. Is Ty here? Did he get Holden yet?" Drew broke off as he stepped into the study. "Oh. Hey, Holden. How are..." he trailed off as Holden made a sound that could only be described as a growl.

"Bunch of busybodies. I don't want your goddamn charity, Cartwright. I'm not a fucking invalid."

"What the hell's going on? He shouldn't be—" Drew said. His last word was lost as Holden shouted at the young vet.

"And I suppose you're in on all of this shit. Did you come here to gloat? You probably think I got what I deserved." His gaze whipped back around to nail Cass to his seat. "I'll be out of here as soon as I can make arrangements. Meanwhile, all of you leave me the fuck alone." He wheeled his way toward the front of the house. Ty hurried after him to hold the doors, leaving Cartwright and Drew staring at each other in an uncomfortable silence.

"Well. That went well," Cass said.

"What went well? What the hell were you thinking? He can't be this upset, he needs time and space to heal. I thought you understood that. Tyler knows damn well—

"Enough, Drew. That was Tyler's idea."

"What? To pick Holden up from the hospital and then give him a heart attack?"

Cass raked his fingers through his hair trying to throttle back some of the tension of the last few minutes. "Ty said the very worst part of his recovery was loosing his place, of not belonging to something he thought he'd do his whole life. He said when he realized, *really understood*, that he couldn't go back to active duty, he got so angry it nearly drove him over the edge. He suggested we give Holden some place to belong and somewhere to focus his anger." Cass swallowed hard. "I don't know if it was worse watching Holden or thinking about Tyler going through that alone."

Drew stood looking out the window while they waited for Ty to return from helping Holden settle in to his new place.

The front door closed with a bang and a few seconds later Ty entered. He cast a quick glance at Drew then moved straight for his lover. Unable to find the words he wanted to say, Cass just folded Tyler against his chest and held him.

Chapter Two

At lunch the next day, Drew looked around the dining room and saw the usual assortment of ranch hands, but no Holden.

Cass sat at the head of the table, eating and talking with the men about fences and cattle and other ranch-related issues. Tyler stood watching over the crew and replenishing the food on the platters and in bowls, making sure that the men were well-fueled for the afternoon chores.

Ty was a former cook in the Navy, both before and after his SEAL training, and Drew knew he preferred to feed everyone and push them back out the door before he ate his own lunch—usually munching while he was cleaning up and starting the preparations for dinner.

He joined Ty near the sideboard where they could speak quietly without being overheard. "No Holden?"

"Hey, Drew. No, he's fully into his pity party at the moment. Don't worry, I made sure he was okay and brought him food."

"Don't you think the man is entitled to feel a little sorry for himself?"

"I know he's better off if someone isn't willing to tiptoe around his black moods. This is his life, now. He's going to have to find a way to deal. You and Cass have to trust me on this."

"You still have to go to Kingman this afternoon?"

"The rest of the appointments are in the morning but it was the only way I could get him in to meet Perry, too."

There was a general commotion as the men finished their meal and filed through to the kitchen to load their plates into the dishwasher.

"Hey, why don't you grab your lunch and come sit with me before I have to head back out," Cass called out from the now empty table, patting the seat next to his.

Drew and Tyler filled their plates and sat.

"Did you come to check on Holden?" Cass asked.

"Yes, well, no. Not really. I mean yes but..." he trailed off as the other two men began to laugh. "Okay, yes, I wanted to know how he was doing, but I actually have another question to ask. And I hope we're good enough friends that you two will be completely honest with me."

Cass sat back and laced his fingers behind his head and waited. Tyler kept eating but shifted his attention to look at Drew.

"So...I came by to tell you this last night but the drama with Holden sort of put it out of my head until I'd already started back. Old Doc Foster's decided he wants to quit trawling the back roads, so we've decided to split. I'm now the proud owner of my own practice, and I'll focus on the western half of the county. We'll still cover each other in emergencies, there will probably be some cross over...but I did it! It's my very own business." He beamed at the other two men.

Tyler high-fived him across the table, but Cass was frowning.

"What about the ranch-owners? Won't they have any say in which doctor they choose?"

Drew's stomach dropped. That had been a concern, but he'd thought Cass liked the way he cared for the stock. He'd been counting on his support. "Well, of course. Ranchers are free to choose any vet they want. You'll receive a formal notification explaining all of this, Cass. Doc Foster doesn't want to leave Kingman anymore and is switching to an office-based practice. We can recommend another large animal vet if you prefer." He couldn't help the stiff tone and he really wished he hadn't taken quite so much food.

Tyler elbowed Cass hard in the side. "Knock it off."

Cass grinned and leaned forward to grab Drew's hand in a hard, two-fisted handshake. "Congratulations, Drew. I'm only kidding. We'd already switched to only asking you to come to the ranch months ago. You have our support and if you need a reference, just ask."

"Thanks," he said. Suddenly he was ravenous, and bit off a large chunk of his sandwich.

"So this is big news, what do you need from us? How can we help?" Cass asked.

Tyler just grinned. He had a feeling his friend already knew what he was going to ask.

"There's not much sense in having an office and living in Kingman, because most of my time is on the ranches and farms. So I'm looking for a small place on this side of the county to live and work. Until I can make that happen, I could use a spot in one of your bunk houses on those nights it's too late to drive back to town."

"Can you and Holden manage to get along? Because you need to know, he's going to be staying out here for a while," Ty said.

"Really? Long term? Somehow I thought it was just for a few days. What about his job? His physical therapy?" Drew asked.

Cass stood and moved to the sideboard to fill his coffee from the ever-present urn. He looked at Drew. "What's the deal between the two of you?"

Drew shrugged. He felt the flush that crept up his neck. "No deal. It's nothing"

"Come on. This goes back before Ty and I even met Holden. Before the cattle poisoning and his trips to the ranch. Obviously that wasn't the first time the two of you had a run-in. How did the two of you meet?"

Drew blew out a breath.

"Tell him, Drew. Cass should know if you're both going to be staying here," Ty said.

Cass raised one eyebrow at his lover. "Keeping secrets?"

Ty shrugged one shoulder and looked uncomfortable. "It wasn't my story to tell."

"Aw, hell, Ty. I didn't mean you couldn't tell Cass." Drew looked between the two men, then shook his head. "It's not a big deal. I met Holden a time or two in town when he first took the job as sheriff. Professional functions. I thought he was hot, but a little standoffish. I wasn't sure he was gay until I ran into him at a club in Laughlin. I asked him to dance, he told me to go fuck myself, that I had the wrong idea. I didn't have the wrong idea, but I did get the message."

"No, I don't think you got it wrong, Drew, but don't tell me you can't understand. Consider his position, not to mention his race and he was new to the area. There was a lot of potential harm if you had bad intentions."

"I get it. But I'm not in the closet and never will be. So yes, I get it, but I hate that anyone feels that way." He looked over at Ty. "Sorry, man. I know you lived that way, too. I was just lucky that I never had to. Mom never made it an issue for me, and I never did either."

"Does he know you saved his life?" Cass asked.

"Nope and he'd probably hate me even more than he already does if he knew. I'd prefer if neither of you mentioned it to him."

"Yeah, you're probably right. I can't promise he won't find out. Enough people know, but he won't hear it from me," Cass said.

Ty nodded absently toward Cass and rose to start clearing the dishes.

"So, about that occasional spot in the bunk house?"

Cass took a swallow of his coffee, raised it in a mock toast. "Drew, it's great news about your solo practice. And you're right, if you pick up the western end of the practice it makes no sense to have an apartment in town, although a young, single guy like yourself might find it a little isolated to work from your own ranch out here."

"Seriously? You are *not* implying that there's a nightlife for anyone in Kingman, let alone a gay man..." Drew grinned.

Cass laughed. "No. You got that right. Besides, you're a little closer to Laughlin from here. No, I really do think you're making a good move, business-wise. There's nothing available the size you're looking for out here right now, but something will open up. Meanwhile, dump your apartment and move into the other casita. Just bring your shit out anytime."

*

Sliding his forearm into the metal support band of the crutches, Holden muscled his way across the floor toward the front window of his casita. He knew Ty would give him hell if he caught him using the wheelchair again tonight. In fact, he should probably just put the damned chair away and focus on building back his strength. He looked across at the main house and realized all the repairs to the kitchen must have taken place during the last two months while he'd been in the hospital and the rehab facility. He'd read the reports and knew the kitchen had been completely destroyed in the blast, but he still remembered nothing surrounding the explosion. It was probably a blessing he didn't remember anything, since he'd been bombarded with pieces of the granite countertop, including catching large pieces in his lower back and legs. He'd been told that if he'd been hit just an inch to the left, he'd have likely severed his spine and never walked again. So, yes, he knew he needed to work his mangled legs, but it was a mystery why the goddamn physical therapist thought it was a good idea to tell Hardin about the daily exercise regimen. Everyone seemed to be treating Holden's injuries like he was some sort of war hero. Tyler was the real deal, Purple Heart, Medal of Honor kind of shit. Poor old Sheriff Titus was just in the wrong place at the wrong time.

Taking the top law enforcement position in the western part of Arizona had been a risk, but settling in Kingman had been the first step in taking control of his life and now ironically, he was starting over—again. Giving himself a mental shake, Holden knew he needed to do something...anything to keep from sitting here by himself thinking about the night his world blew apart. There were decisions to be made, plans to formulate.

Opening his laptop, he pulled up the spreadsheet that contained his life... all of his account information, income, expenditures, savings, retirement. There was going to be a small disability pension, but it wouldn't be enough to meet all of his obligations.

Shit. He closed the file in frustration. Half the reason he'd moved to Kingman in the first place was to establish a residence in an affordable community. He was going to have to do something in the short term while he finished the physical therapy. Then he'd know more about his own physical limitations and could make some long-term arrangements. *God knows I don't think I will survive if I have to move back to Southern California.* For now, he needed to figure out how he could find a job that paid enough to afford his own a small place near medical care and cover his other expenses.

Three hours later, Holden was thoroughly frustrated. He'd scanned the online classifieds for the entire tri-state region. Where there were jobs there was no affordable housing. Cheap apartments seemed to equal no jobs. For now, he was going to have to accept Cass's offer of a temporary job and place to live. He shut everything down and closed his laptop. The snick of the latch felt full of meaning. As if he were closing the lid on the life he'd briefly allowed himself to believe was possible.

With clumsy limbs and a bone weariness that went deeper than the workout from his physical therapy, he made his way outside. Warm air caressed his skin and he breathed deeply of the summer desert night.

Casita. Holden couldn't even think the word without an internal snort. Mi casa es su casa and all that. It wasn't that he didn't appreciate everything Cass was doing for him, but he'd taken the job as sheriff and moved to a new state in order to follow his own dreams. Now his future seemed further away than ever before. How had he been so fucking wrong?

Chapter Three

The desk had been moved to the side of the room and Holden noticed all the throw rugs had been removed. He assumed the changes were in deference to his new, less than prime physical condition. He was embarrassed by how heavy he sounded as he half collapsed into the leather office chair. Cass prevented the chair from rolling with a subtle shift of his foot behind the wheel. Then he slid an open folder across the smooth oak surface.

"I'll be right back with some coffee for both of us. Look this over and see if we need to make any changes."

When the coffee was on the desk and Cass seated in the chair next to him, Holden pointed at the first folder.

"A contract?"

"Protects all parties involved," Cass replied. "This is more than a casual agreement between friends, Titus. I know it's not the same as being the sheriff or even a cop of any sort, but it's important to me. To the whole group. We've formed a consortium; my attorney drew up the paperwork. If you want to have it checked by your own attorney, you go ahead. Before you sign, you should make sure you're going to have everything you need. We've established a baseline budget, but didn't have all of the details for what you think you might need to do the job."

Holden frowned. "This says I'm working for Willow Springs Ranch," he said pointing at the contract. "I don't want your charity—"

"Shut up, Holden. There are several pages, read the whole thing before you start getting all pissy with me again. WSR is your employer, however, much of your salary and the work will be coming from the consortium. The rest of your time will be spent on projects I need done for the ranch.

"Room and board are included," Cass held up a hand before Holden could object. "Comes with every job here, so get over that. Here are the first background checks we need done. We weren't sure what you would need, so this first batch is sort of sketchy. We want to do it all electronic, so you'll have to figure it out. Keep in mind, we're just a bunch of cowboys, so simple is good.

"I need to get out to the upper forty, so I'm going to leave you all these and the contract. Read it over and write down your questions. We can meet after lunch. Ty's in the kitchen, but he's dying for me to get out of here so he can come check on you."

Holden gave a little snort, his mind already going to how to set up a computerized database to track the requests. The big hand on his shoulder surprised him and he looked up. Cass seemed to hesitate, then appeared to change whatever it had been he was going to say. "Get your list together for anything you need and update me. You and Ty can get it tomorrow when you're in town." He gave a comforting squeeze then loped out the door. Holden barely noticed, he was already focused on the files.

*

Drew pulled his pick up into the dirt yard between the two casitas. He tried not to stare at the windows of Holden's place, but he couldn't resist a quick peek as he climbed from the truck. The windows looked back, blankly impassive and opaque in the mid-afternoon glare.

He allowed himself a momentary thought of living here more permanently, surrounded by a group of men who didn't give a rat's ass that he was gay. Cass and Ty were out and a couple on their own compound, but not everyone on the ranch was gay. The rule was you had to be tolerant. He'd been warned about possible backlash when he'd first accepted a position in this part of Arizona. It wasn't the most liberal of states, that was for sure. But he'd found the folks who lived and ranched along the I-40 corridor to be a fiercely independent group. They hated to be told how to live their lives and so resisted any outward judgments. Not that Drew flaunted his sexuality, but he had made it clear enough. When he'd first started at the Golden Valley Animal Hospital straight out of college, Dr.

Foster had grinned at the parade of women who suddenly decided their dogs and cats needed to update their shots. One by one Drew had gently informed each of the women he wasn't interested. A few had assumed he just hadn't met the right woman yet, but most accepted him. One woman had even tried to set him up with her brother.

With a box tucked under his arm, Drew opened the door to his temporary home. He was half a step across the threshold before it registered that something was very wrong. The place was supposed to be partially furnished, but everything was stacked to one side and covered in paint-splattered drop clothes. All of the blinds and curtains were removed, a ladder leaned against the wall, and a large table saw was balanced on two sawhorses. *What the fuck?*

"Hey," said a soft-voiced youth kneeling on the floor. There were blueprints and a floor plan spread out on the tile in front of the blond-haired, blue-eyed cutie.

"Hi. Uhm…I think you might be in the wrong spot. I'm supposed to be staying here. Maybe you got the wrong casita?"

"Nope. I spent an hour with Ty this morning. This is where I'm supposed to be working. I'm going to be renovating and making major repairs for a couple of months. You're Drew, right? My name's Chad, nice to meet you."

He sighed. "Yep, I'm Drew and I guess I need to take my stuff elsewhere."

"It's cool, Drew. Ty has it all worked out. He said I needed to get all this work done so you can have a nice place to live when I'm finished. He's got a place for you to stay. Check with Ty."

With apparently little choice in the matter, Drew stepped back into the yard and found Ty waiting for him next to the bed of his truck.

"I guess I was a little premature in letting my apartment go," Drew said. He heard the tightness in his voice but didn't apologize. It was all well and good for Ty to stand there grinning. He had a place to live. As of three hours ago, Drew was homeless. "I guess Cass didn't mean it literally when he said I was welcome anytime." His phone buzzed before Ty could respond and Drew held up a hand for the other man to wait while he took a call. He checked the digital display. Doc Foster.

"Van..."

"Drew? Can you cover McCallister's for me? Mille, their Australian Shepard is dropping her litter and Old Mac says she's in distress. I thought since you were out that way it would save the time of them driving her in. He's pretty worked up about it. He loves that dog."

Drew checked his watch, looked at the back of the truck loaded down with boxes and heaved another sigh. "Yeah, I've got it. Looks like my other plans fell through anyway. I'll call and let you know."

Hooking his phone back on his belt, Drew said, "Look, I know Cass said no bunkhouse, but I really could use a place to crash tonight, then I'll be out of your hair tomorrow."

"No need. After Cass offered the place up last night I came and looked around. It wasn't fit for a person to live in. A night or two, sure, but not to move in long-term. This is the place Gibby and Roy shared..." He trailed off and swallowed hard.

Drew knew that was a hard memory for Ty to think of the loss of the man who'd been more than a friend. Gibby had been Ty's surrogate father, and the one who'd invited Ty to the Willow Springs Ranch. And died an hour before Ty arrived.

"Chad is the son of an old friend and was already here, working as a handy man for a few days while he sorts through what to do next. Put himself through college as a laborer on construction sites, so we asked him to stick around to fix this place up."

"College? The kid looks like he needs to get back to high school."

"Hah," Ty said. "He's older than he looks. Has his Masters in Education. It's a long story. Let's just say that for now, he'd like some time to think and manual labor gives him the freedom he wants. Now, you can stay here with Chad. Of course there's no kitchen and no furniture. You'd probably have to bunk on the floor."

Drew narrowed his eyes...Ty was up to something. "I'm not interested—"

Ty cut him off. "Or you can stay in the other casita with Holden. Now don't look at me in that tone of voice. It would only be for a little while, until Chad gets your place fixed up. There are two bedrooms with two baths. Plenty of room for two men as a temporary

33

solution. And whenever you bring out the rest of your stuff, we can put it in storage until the other place is free."

"Well, shit. You're turning into a regular little matchmaker, aren't you? I've got to run. Mac's dog Millie needs a hand. I'll figure something out. All the rest of my stuff is already in storage—my place in Kingman was furnished. Meanwhile, can I stack these boxes someplace before I take off?"

"Yep. We'll put them in the spare room in Holden's place."

Drew rolled his eyes, but quickly stacked two boxes and carried them inside. He scanned the room and headed for the closed door on a guess that was the spare room. Pushing it open, he found a comfortable looking room with a double bed and small sitting area with a television. He put his boxes on the floor and headed back to unload the rest of his things. He could do this. It would probably only be for a couple of weeks. Plus, if he offered to help Chad with the renovations, things would move more quickly. He pretended the work of unloading was solely responsible for the increase in his pulse rate. It was definitely not at the thought of staying in the same house as Holden.

With his hand on the door to his truck, Drew turned and found his friend watching him, his bright blue eyes squinting against the late afternoon glare.

"What?" he asked.

"You don't have to do this. When you get back tonight I'll put you up in the main house and we can sort it all out tomorrow."

"I'm just not sure why you think it's a good idea, Ty. You know how he feels about me."

"I know what *you* think he feels. I'm not convinced you're right. Look, there's a reason I'd like you to stay there, I admit it. At least for a couple of weeks. Keep an eye on him, get him to talk about things. You're not a nursemaid and you keep shitty hours, so you won't be around much anyway. I was just hoping for another pair of eyes. The first few weeks out of the hospital can be brutal. If something else comes of it—great, if not, you'd still be helping me."

"Shit," Drew said. He raked his fingers through his hair and looked back toward the small house. Stalling for time, searching for an answer. Holden had fascinated him from the moment he'd first laid eyes on the man. He'd had more than one fantasy of running his tongue over all that beautiful chestnut-colored skin. With his close-cropped black hair and eyes so dark they were nearly black, the man was sex on a stick. But Holden was deep in the closet and Drew wouldn't go there. Not for anyone.

Trying to block the temptation to say yes, Drew blew out a breath and closed his eyes. He was immediately hit with an unwelcome memory of his own hands covered in blood as he'd rhythmically pumped, working and praying he could keep Holden alive until they got him to a hospital. He opened his

35

eyes, climbed into the truck, and shut the door. Admitting defeat, he lowered the window.

"Okay. I'll give it a try. But promise me I can have a room at the big house if it gets too bad. "

Chapter Four

"Dinner is ready. Are you planning on joining us or did you think you had to work all night?" Ty asked.

Holden looked up, and blinked to clear his eyes. "Shit. What time is it?" He looked at his watch, even as Ty answered.

"Dinner time. Seven. Come on, you've been at this all day."

"Can I just get a plate to take back? My ass is dragging."

"Yeah, I figured you'd say that. Come on back through the kitchen on your way out. I'll have it wrapped up. Did your first day go okay?"

"Actually, it did. But you knew that already." He surprised himself with a laugh. "How many times do you think you stuck your head in to check on me today?"

Ty smiled and shook his head. "No idea. I tried not to bother you."

"You didn't. Hey, thanks." He pointed in the direction of the desk with his chin as he wrapped the metal bands of the crutches around his forearms. "This was better. Better than sitting in the rehab. But I'm wiped. We have an early trip to Kingman in the morning. I'm going to go veg in front of the TV and go to sleep early."

"Yeah, about your place...you should know that—"

"Nope. Not another word, Tyler. You're not going to convince me to stay for dinner. I need some peace and quiet. Now, go get that food and put it in a bag while I figure out how to make my damn legs move again."

He pushed himself to his feet and struggled for a minute to get his limbs untangled. After sitting all day in one position his legs felt like cooked spaghetti. He was supposed to get up and move every hour, put weight on his legs and make the muscles work. Well, tomorrow was another day. One in which he could count on the torture of physical therapy to remind him of today's failures.

Giving the ranch hands a wide berth, Holden moved in a herky-jerky fashion through the kitchen, wrapped the handles of the canvas grocery bag around his wrist and moved through the door while Ty was busy setting out the massive platters of food.

The walk from the kitchen door to the casita was a long, flat path. Nothing he would have considered strenuous before the bomb, but his elevated heart rate and shaky muscles felt like he was on the back end of a marathon.

"Sheriff Titus?"

He tried to turn and lost his balance. He'd have gone over if a strong hand hadn't grabbed his arm. "Fuck. Are you trying to give me a heart attack, Juan?" The ranch hand who'd been so helpful during the investigation of the cattle poisoning looked at him with big dark eyes.

"I'm sorry. I didn't mean to…uhm…Sheriff—" he repeated, then broke off and looked away. Holden's cop-sense went on alert.

"I'm not the sheriff any more, Juan. If you need the law, you need to call Sheriff Morgan."

"No. I can't. This is…outside the law."

Intrigued, Holden led the way to the split rail fence that surrounded the kitchen garden, and leaned against the top rail. "What is it? You in some kind of trouble?"

"Not me. My cousin, Enrique. He…uhm…can I tell you this? I don't know who else to go to…"

"Sounds like you need to tell someone. I'm not a lawyer or a priest, so I can't promise to keep your secret, but if there's anything I can do to help, I will. Why don't you tell me what's on your mind?"

"My cousin Enrique is missing. He was coming to pick up some work over in the valley, but he never made it here."

"He coming legally?"

Juan shook his head and Holden sighed. It was a pervasive problem in this part of the country. "Coyote? Or is he by himself?"

"I loaned him the money to pay for the trip. I told him he was stupid, but his Maria is pregnant and he wanted to earn enough to pay for her to stay home instead of going back to her job after the baby comes. He was supposed to get here yesterday or today, but we haven't heard from him. Can you help?"

Paid for his trip. A euphemism that made the journey sound like a vacation. In fact, the trips were fraught with danger, and the outrageous fees charged by the syndicates were no guarantee that the Mexican citizen would make it safely into the US. Some were robbed, the money taken, no trip ever materialized. Others would be smuggled into the back of truck never to be seen or heard from again. It was a damn stupid thing to do. On the other hand, if you understood the lengths that people would go to in order to care for their family, it made total sense.

"All right, Juan. I'm not the sheriff, and you damn well know it, or you wouldn't have asked me for help. So that means you call me Holden. There isn't anything I can do tonight. Tomorrow you call your cousin's wife and see if she's heard anything. Get me all the information you can. Names, departure, arrival locations. Anything. Meet me tomorrow afternoon with everything you've got and I'll see what I can do. Now, I'm done for tonight."

As Juan headed toward the bunkhouse, Holden forced himself back to his feet. He would count himself lucky if he could make it to the door of his casita without falling down. Concentrating on putting one foot in front of the other, leaning heavily on the crutches and banging the bag containing his dinner with every step, Holden finally made it across the yard.

He balanced on shaking legs as he pushed the door open. He swiped a trembling hand over his sweaty face, then blinked rapidly as his brain fought to catch up with what he was seeing.

"What the fuck are you doing here?"

****

Drew noted the ashy grey tone and light coating of sweat over Holden's face and fought the urge to go to the man and help him to the couch. His assistance wouldn't be welcome and in fact would probably make the news of his new roommate even less palatable. Without answering, his eyes narrowed as Holden staggered slightly sideways before dropping heavily into the wheelchair and tossing the crutches and a bag into the corner. He hadn't put any weight on his legs and that wasn't a good thing. If he wanted to recover, the man was going to have to start making an effort.

"Is that how you've been using your crutches all day? You've got to start—"

"Mind your own fucking business. Why are you here? Get lost on your way home?" Holden's voice came out a tired shell of his typical growl, and that alarmed Drew as much as anything.

"I am home. At least temporarily," Drew said, keeping his voice even and calm.

"What the fuck is that supposed to mean?" Holden wheeled himself over to a low counter in the kitchen, and for the first time, Drew realized the cabin was designed to be wheelchair accessible. Wide doorways, low counters, wooden floors, and the furniture placed for maximum access.

Frowning, he watched as Holden opened the refrigerator and got himself a beer. After twisting off the top and taking a long pull from the bottle, he turned his chair to face Drew, clearly waiting for an answer.

"It means Tyler and Cass are letting me bunk here temporarily while the renovations next door are finished. Don't worry, Titus. I'll be out of your hair soon enough."

"Shit." Holden finished off the beer and got another. "Let's be clear on this. You are staying here? In this cabin? With me? Good to know. I'll be moving out tomorrow. Now mind your own fucking business tonight and leave me alone."

"Yes. Well." Drew forced himself not to wince at the thought of the alcohol mixing with the pain meds and hoped the man had already eaten. Then he realized the bag Holden tossed aside probably contained his dinner. Knowing he was messing up, he tried any way. "You know, you should probably eat something. I'll just pick this up," he said, moving to the grocery bag. "Why don't you go in the living room and watch a little TV, and I'll put this on a plate and bring it to you."

"Is that why you're here? To watch over me?" Holden took in a deep breath and Drew braced himself for the explosion. It never came. Instead, the other man's voice sounded as tired as he looked. "I appreciate Ty's concern, there's no doubt this is his doing. It's too late for you to drive back to your own place tonight, but don't bother coming tomorrow. I'm a big boy and I sure as hell don't need another mother. Now if you don't mind, I'm going to just sit on the couch and watch some television. And I'd prefer to do it alone."

At a loss for what to do next, Drew looked toward the front door, half inclined to stay at the main house. Instead, he carried the bag of food to the kitchen. Unpacking what seemed like enough food for three people, he tried not to stare as Holden put word to action and rolled to the living room. He levered himself from the wheelchair to the couch and then used the remote to turn on the Suns game.

Without another word, Drew opened the plastic containers and dished out two plates of meatloaf and pasta, then poured a sauce full of basil and mushrooms over everything. His mouth watered and he thought the growl from his stomach was probably loud enough to frighten the horses in the barn. There was no sense asking Holden if he wanted something to eat. The man would always push him away, but it was beyond Drew to walk away without helping. So he carried a plate of food, utensils, and a glass of water to the living room and placed them on the coffee table in front of Holden. Then he took his dinner into his room, sat in front of his television, eating alone while watching the same basketball game that Holden watched alone in the other room.

*

Drew woke with a start to realize the television was still on and someone had obviously nailed his head on sideways. "Damn," he whispered, as he slowly straightened himself from his slumped position. The silverware clattered to the floor, sending his heart skittering, and he nearly dropped the plate from his lap when he moved his feet from the ottoman. A quick look at his watch revealed he'd been asleep for a couple of hours. *Jesus Christ, sound asleep and drooling before midnight. How attractive is that?*

After retrieving his wayward fork from under the bed, Drew shuffled to the kitchen on bare feet to put his dishes in the dishwasher. The living room television was playing the same infomercial and he realized Holden had fallen asleep on the couch. The now-empty dinner plate on the coffee table pleased him. Making no effort to be quiet, Drew scrubbed, loaded, and started the dishwasher in hopes of waking the other man from where he reclined in an awkward position on the couch.

There was no real choice…he'd have to help him to the bed. Holden would never be able to move tomorrow if he slept with his body twisted and his legs curled sideways. To give himself time and Holden some privacy, just in case he was faking the sleep, Drew returned to his room and went through his evening routine. Pulling on a pair of soft cotton sleeping pants seemed safer than just wandering around in his boxers, but he decided going without a shirt was acceptable in the middle of the night.

Morning came early for a vet in ranch country, and he needed to get back to sleep.

When he'd stalled long enough he stepped back into the living room and saw Holden sitting up, rubbing a hand on his head as he looked around the room with eyes that were heavy with fatigue.

Crossing the room quickly, he spoke softly. "Holden? It's me, Drew. Hang on, let me help you to your room."

Holden looked up, his normally strong face was etched in unfamiliar lines bracketing his mouth. "Drew?" he asked, his brows furrowed in confusion. "Wha's going on? Everything hurts…"

"I know. Come on, let me help you to bed." Lifting one of Holden's arms and draping it around his neck, Drew used his own strong back to power the two of them from the couch. Supporting nearly all of the other man's weight, he moved Holden toward the bedroom, one slow step at a time.

"Need a piss," Holden mumbled.

With a mental eye roll, Drew steered them toward the en suite. When he had Holden positioned in front of the toilet, Drew unfastened the button fly and slid the worn denim down dark muscular legs. *Holy fuck, he goes commando!*

Drew tried to focus on the task, reminding himself this was a lot like treating an injured animal, and not at all like kneeling at the feet of a man whose taste you craved. Lifting one foot at a time, he helped Holden step free of the jeans, so he could get ready for bed when he was finished. Standing quickly, he patted

Holden's bare hip and promised any listening saints that he would not think about this tomorrow.

"I'll hold you up, you do the rest," he said. He rested his head against the warm, broad back and listened to the steady thump of Holden's heart. The heart that had ceased to beat and then returned to life. The heart he wished belonged to him.

"'Kay, I'm done," Holden said. He managed to turn and dropped his arm around Drew's shoulder without prompting. Together they shuffled toward the big bed. After pulling the covers back, Drew turned Holden and lowered him to the edge of the bed and helped get his legs fully onto the mattress.

"Do you have some sleep pants or something?"

"No, don't like the way they make me feel." Holden pulled his shirt over his head and tossed it toward the corner of the room.

Drew swallowed hard. "When's the last time you took your pain meds?"

"After lunch. I don't like the way they make me feel, either."

"I know. I'll be right back."

Back in the kitchen, Drew sorted through the bottles on the counter until he found what he needed and filled a glass with water. He brought the crutches with him when he returned to the bedroom and stood them within easy reach of the bed.

"Here you go, Holden," he said, handing over the tablets and the glass of water. "You should sleep the rest of the night. I'm going to leave the bedroom doors open, just in case. I'm a light sleeper, I'll hear if you call my name." He held his hand out for the glass and then placed it on the bedside table.

"Scoot on down and I'll pull up the sheet," he said, reluctant to leave the intimacy of the moment. They were surrounded by the dark, alone in a way they'd never been before, and seeing the normally gruff Holden Titus so vulnerable left Drew feeling protective.

Raising the covers, he watched as Holden settled back against the pillows. When the other man closed strong fingers around his wrist and tugged, Drew leaned down. Expecting a whispered thanks, he was unprepared for the soft brush of lips. He would have pulled back, but Holden wrapped a big hand around the nape of his neck and pulled him closer, pressing their mouths together. Drew opened his mouth to say…something, anything, but before his brain could fully form any words, Holden's tongue swept into his mouth.

The slick heat of the kiss was as delicious as it was unexpected and Drew allowed himself to be drawn in, to taste, to savor the moment. Then the unwelcome reality of the moment washed over him. Holden was drugged, still hurting, and feeling vulnerable. This was neither the time nor the place.

He cupped Holden's face in his hands and slowed the pace of the kiss, until he could pull back. He pressed one more kiss to the sculpted mouth, the tip of nose, the broad forehead. "Good night, Holden. I'll be gone early, so I'll see you tomorrow night. Sleep well."

Chapter Five

Two days ago Holden had spent the day nailed to the office desk in the main house as he put the details of his new job together. Yesterday had been busy with the long drive to and from physical therapy. He didn't mind long hours, but wasn't sure his career in law enforcement prepared him for a nine-to-five type of desk job. Yet that was exactly what this position with Cass looked to morph into. Not the hours, of course, because everything on a ranch started much earlier than nine. It was more the sitting-behind-the-computer all day that was getting to him. With a quick glance at his watch, Holden discovered he'd been hunched over the keyboard nearly two hours. He needed to put some parameters around his time or risk another total collapse at the end of the day.

Today he was working from his kitchen instead of the office in the main house. There were calls he wanted to make on Juan's behalf and he could use a little break from Ty's happy interference. Not that he really minded, but if he had to endure one more casually dropped hint about Drew's perfection…attractive…good veterinarian…so smart… He touched his fingers to his lips and smiled. No doubt Ty would love to hear what a good kisser Drew was, too, but that information would be better kept to himself.

Not that Holden was in the closet. He wasn't. He just kept all of his personal business where it should be. Personal. He assumed Cass and Tyler knew…but maybe he should tell them. Drew thought he knew. Aww…fuck. Who was he kidding? Drew knew.

Brewing a fresh pot of coffee, Holden used the time to stretch out his back and legs and remember that night in the club in Laughlin. Not that it had been anything particularly special. A little hole in the wall sort of place that club served the tri-state area, set at the Needles end of the strip. He should have realized he'd run in to someone but he'd just been so damned relieved to find there was someplace he might go to meet other men occasionally that he hadn't been thinking…straight. He laughed out loud at his own thought and poured a cup of coffee.

Straight. Without a bend or angle. Well, he was definitely bent, he supposed. He'd come to that knowledge a little later in life than so many gay men he'd spoken to over the years. Had it been denial or more of a gentle evolution? It didn't really matter. He was at a time in life when he'd needed a new start for many reasons, and the Kingman job had popped up first. Naturally he'd looked for some entertainment and ended up at the club in Laughlin. He'd just wanted a little anonymous fun while everything in his life was up in the air. Instead, he'd found himself facing the one man in town he couldn't afford to get close to until he had his life in order. He'd only been a few weeks away from getting everything organized according to his plan when the world had blown apart.

"Hey. Working from here today?"

Startled, Holden turned toward the second bedroom. Drew stood, perfectly framed in the doorway, sleep tousled and dreamy. His brownish-blond hair was at war with itself, flat on one side and sticking up at odd angles on the other. Amber eyes, usually bright with intelligence or mischief, were swollen and tired-looking. With his two-day growth of beard and just-got-out-of bed look, it was about all Holden could do not to turn the man around and bundle him back onto the mattress that would still be warm. Then he remembered his crutches.

Leaning his ass against the kitchen counter, Holden blew over the surface of the life-sustaining liquid before he took a careful sip. "Yes…well giving working from home a try. Sorry, did I wake you? I didn't realize you'd be here still."

"Mmm…is that coffee? 'Cause I'd give just about anything for a tall black cop…shit…cup." A slow flush crept up the creamy skin of Drew's neck as he crossed the room toward the kitchen.

Unsure whether to be more flattered or amused, Holden reached for a second mug and poured. Their fingers brushed as he handed the cup to Drew, and for a moment, the two of them stood inches apart in the small kitchen, their gazes locked. Drew looked away first and moved to the other side of the counter.

"Yes...well. I was out late. Jergen's thoroughbred foaled and it was a long night. It was touch and go for a while. And no, you didn't wake me. I set my alarm. I have to get back and check on mother and baby before I take on my afternoon appointments."

"All right. I was just about to cook some eggs. Want some before you go?"

"Uhm...sure. If it's not too much trouble. You can cook?"

Holden laughed at the incredulous tone of the younger man's voice. "Well, I'm not as good as Tyler, but yeah, I can throw a few things together." As he spoke, he set the cast iron skillet on the burner, then pulled a package of bacon and a carton of eggs from the refrigerator. He rummaged around and got the rest of the ingredients he wanted lined up on the counter. While the bacon started to sizzle, he chopped and prepped veggies for an omelet. Drew's gaze at his back made him self-conscious as he shifted his weight between the counter and his crutches while he worked.

"You move pretty good around this kitchen. It's a nice set up," Drew observed.

Relieved to have something to talk about, Holden quickly agreed. "It's the same set up they're putting in your place. There's a third unfinished casita that will be next, then Ty says they plan to build a few more."

"Really? What the hell does Cass need with all these casitas? Ranch hands don't stick around long enough to need much more than a bunk house."

Holden laughed. "Well, it seems Cass has run into the infectious enthusiasm of a born do-gooder. Do you know about the week-long camp Cass holds every year for disabled kids?"

When Drew nodded, he continued. "Ty made some remark on Tuesday that he wished there was something similar for gay kids and kids with gay parents. A place they could go without worrying about bullying or sticking out. So here we are on Thursday, and the plans are fully underway. He talked about it all the way to Kingman and back yesterday."

"Ah…finding a few minutes of quiet is the real reason you're working from home instead of the big house today."

"Exactly." He nodded. "Now there's a contractor coming today to look over the place and to see if he can modify the existing plans, in case they want to build two wheelchair accessible dorms."

Drew laughed. "Damn. No wonder you stayed home. Oh, hey. You weren't kidding," he said. "That smells delicious."

"Good. Now you come get the plates and silverware and set us up at the counter while I start another pot of coffee. Then everything will be ready."

The two men worked companionably for a minute in the small kitchen, and Holden tried not to think of how he'd kissed Drew the other night…or of how Drew had drawn back.

"Mmm…definitely delicious. I nominate you as official chef while we live together."

Blinking rapidly, Holden swallowed a bite of bacon unchewed and nearly choked. When he could speak, he said, "We aren't living together."

"Are too…and you're the cook. I'll clean up. I hate to clean, but we'd be eating Pop-Tarts if I was making breakfast."

Frowning, Holden finished his breakfast and tried to ignore how often Drew managed to brush against his arm, his leg. Or the smell of the man. *Damn it.* Breakfast together at the counter was a bit more intimate than he'd imagined. He just hadn't wanted to clean up his workspace at the table. And despite the flirtatiousness of the light touches, he couldn't—wouldn't—forget that Drew had pulled back.

*

Sitting next to Holden, having breakfast together was more than Drew had ever let himself imagine. Sure he'd thought about sex with the prickly sheriff, but never once in all his fantasies had he imagined the morning after. Yet here they were, sharing a small counter, hip-to-hip, just like a regular couple. Except of course for the part about them having sex, since they hadn't. Yet, he amended.

Unable to delay the inevitable workday any longer, he brushed his hand over Holden's broad back, and reached for his plate with the other. "I've got the dishes. Then I'm afraid duty calls."

Standing at the sink rinsing the dishes made it easy to unobtrusively watch as Holden crossed to the dining table, still putting most of his weight on the crutches. That wasn't good. He needed to make those legs work before the muscles atrophied more from the lack of use. Drew thought he should talk with the physical therapist, himself. He had no doubt there were exercises Holden was supposed to do between appointments.

Finished with the dishes, he moved to the table and again brushed his hand over Holden's back. "Thanks for breakfast. I'm gonna shower before I leave for work," he said. With a gentle squeeze of the heavily muscled shoulder, Drew swallowed the invitation that hovered on his lips. *Damn.*

*

Drew bit back a moan after adjusting the water to spray across his own tense shoulders. God he was wound tight. It might have something to do with that chocolately goodness sitting at the kitchen table. Not that there was anything sweet about the taste he'd gotten from their kiss the other night. No, the man was like a dark, drugging spice, teasing his senses, seducing him into a hunger, a need, that left him feeling stupid and inept. Asking for a tall black cop instead of a cup. Shit. At least Holden had looked amused instead of angry. In fact, the man seemed to be settling in, more comfortable around Drew. Unfortunately, despite all the light touches this morning, Holden hadn't seemed eager to kiss him again. Did he even remember the kiss they'd shared?

Drew had been hoping for a reprisal, but it looked as if he was going to have to chalk that experience up to a late night and pain medication. Too bad, because it had been a very fine kiss.

Lightly skimming his hand over his chest, Drew pinched a nipple and his dick went from interested to hot-damn-I'm-ready-now. Closing his eyes, he followed the trail of hair that ran from his navel to the trimmed patch at the base of his cock. With his pulse rate nicely elevated, Drew held off his pleasure, taking care of the business of getting clean first. Once his hair was shampooed, he reached for the crème rinse. He filled his hand with a fair amount, turned the showerhead to the side, so it wasn't spraying directly on him, and leaned his back against the side of the stall. Wrapping his fist around the base of his dick, he let the slick motion work its magic. With his eyes closed he had a perfect vision of Holden on his knees, sculpted dark lips stretched wide around the base of his cock and imagined that his hard thrusts went to the back of a willing throat.

****

Holden tried to check his temper. Although he could speak enough Spanish to make an arrest, he couldn't keep up with the rapid-fire answers on the other end of the phone. It would be hours before Juan returned to translate for him, and he wanted these answers now. Juan's cousin Enrique had officially been reported as missing, but still only on the Mexican side of the border. There was no evidence that he could find that Enrique had crossed into the US. He'd finally managed to track down the lead investigator in Nogales, but now they were stymied by their inability to communicate.

"*Si, si, pero no hablo español. ¿Habla inglés?*" he asked, falling back on the formal phrase.

"Here, give me the phone, Holden," Drew said from behind him. "Tell me what you want to know."

They exchanged information, then Drew asked the questions and relayed the answers, and made notes on Holden's pad of paper. After a few minutes, he recognized the tone of the end of a conversation.

"Anything else, Holden?"

"No, thank him for me and make sure we have the contact information, in case there's an easier way to reach him."

As Drew ended the call, Holden was pouring over the notes, trying to decipher the cramped writing. "Okay, I need a second translation, here," he said pointing to the yellow legal pad. "What the hell does this say?"

"What? You don't read doctor?" Drew asked. His grin was wide. "Sorry, I know, I know. My mother despairs of me, trust me. She said if I wasn't going to learn penmanship, then I had to be a doctor. I wasn't interested in sick people or in handwriting, so we compromised and I became a veterinarian."

"Ha...makes perfect sense. Now spell this so I get it right."

"E-S-P-I-N-O-Z-A. That's the name of the man on the Arizona side of Nogales who is supposedly the contact for the people who are looking to cross into the US for a fee. Torres said he's working the angle from his side, but he's reluctant to give the name over to the Immigration folks, but I convinced him you're not a cop." His face lost his habitual smile. "I'm sorry, Holden. I had to tell him that or he never would have given me the information. Fortunately, I went to school with a veterinarian from his side of Nogales and her cousin knows his brother, so now Torres thinks of us as family."

The pain in Holden's chest at the loss of his career made it hard to breathe for a minute. He nodded, forced himself to write. When he could speak again, he said, "Okay. Thanks for this, Drew. I don't know what I can do with the information, but it's definitely more than I would have gotten without you."

"Yeah. Sorry," Drew repeated. "Do you want to tell me what this is about? I take it Juan has a cousin who crossed the border illegally?"

"Yeah, he paid some coyotes and no one knows where he is. And you've got nothing to be sorry for; that was the truth. I'm not a cop. It just takes a little getting used to, that's all. Now get out so I can get some work done," he said. Because he had an irresistible urge to put a smile back on Drew's handsome face he added, "Don't forget to take that travel mug with you. I filled it with some tall, black...to go."

Chapter Six

Drew shook off his misgivings about violating Holden's privacy, not to mention every rule and law governing patient confidentiality. He hadn't been kidding when he'd mentioned considering becoming a doctor at one point. He'd spent much of his early college years in pre-med. He'd taken classes on physiology and had enough experience in working with the humans who belonged to his patients to recognize when medical advice was being ignored. Tyler had brought Holden to the ranch less than a week ago, yet the former sheriff insisted his physical therapy was reduced to two-days a week. Something didn't ring true about that. Plus Holden wasn't putting any weight on his legs. He sat at the damn desk or kitchen table all day and used his massive arms to muscle himself around on his aluminum crutches. Not right.

Since he had no plans to get himself or anyone else in trouble he would let the situation determine which way to play it once he was inside. With a hard swallow against nerves, he reminded himself this was for a good reason, to force that stubborn man to comply with his treatment.

Drew parked in front of the ranch style building and wondered who had been in charge of selecting the bright yellow paint. Was it a paint chip gone wild or had someone wanted the building visible from outer space? Pushing his way through the glass doors, it quickly became obvious the look was intentional. Lime green, flamingo pink, and electric aquamarine warred with the virulent yellow to make the small waiting room vibrate like a neon rainbow.

Every head in the crowded waiting room followed his progress to the reception counter. He'd gambled that arriving during the busiest time of the day might net him the results he wanted. With any luck he could be in and out before anyone figured out he had no real authority.

Strolling confidently toward the gum-smacking twenty-something working the window, he put every bit of authority he could muster into his voice. "Dr. Andrew Van," he said waving his laminated staff identification for the University School of Veterinary Medicine. Quickly tucking the card away before someone actually tried to read it, he continued. "I need to see the treatment protocol for patient Holden Titus. I'm due in surgery shortly, so a copy would be best." Technically, he hadn't lied.

"Oh, uhm, could you wait? Uh, Mrs. Lucroy stepped out and Sil is out sick, and I, uhm—"

With an inward wince at his rudeness, he cut her off. "I appreciate your dilemma, I really do, but I just can't wait. How about this? If you can just make a quick copy of the treatment sheet, I can get what I need and be on my way. And if you'd make sure to write your name on the copy, I'll see to it that you get the recognition you deserve for helping me in this important matter."

"I don't..." she trailed off. Her gaze shifted over his shoulder as the front door opened. He could see the familiar red and white van from the Veteran's Assistance Society parked in the drive. The driver pushed in an elderly man in a wheelchair, while two other men waited to be moved inside. The woman grew more flustered as she realized more patients were arriving.

"Looks like you're about to get busy," he said, drawing her attention back to his request. "Last name is T-I-T-U-S. If you could just make a quick copy, I've got that surgery..."

*

Flipping back the top sheet that detailed the physician's recommendations, Drew turned directly to the therapist's notes. He felt the flush in his face as he read the terse comments and sparse notations. He slapped the evidence of Holden's non-compliance on the passenger seat of his truck, then counted to ten before huffing out a breath. Looking up, he saw the clinic door open and an older woman wearing a leopard print pair of scrubs shaded her eyes and scanned the lot. The previously absent Mrs. Lucroy, he presumed. Deliberately ignoring her frantic waves in his direction, he looked over his shoulder and backed out of his parking space. It wouldn't do to hit a car in the crowded lot. Or to be questioned about illegally obtaining medical records…because, joy of joys, he still had a two hour drive and a cow's bowel to repair. Could this day get any better? *Oh wait…I'll have another ass to take care of when I get home….*

****

The steady buzz of the kitchen timer reminded him it was time to get up and do his leg exercises. Unfortunately, if he took the scheduled twenty-minute stretching break now, he'd probably miss the NPS law enforcement ranger he was trying to reach. And since the conversation was related to the missing illegal immigrant and not the job he was being paid to do by Cass, he needed to take care of it on his own time.

Wincing as he straightened his stiff legs, Holden hefted himself from the table. He used his arms to support his weight and leaned on the counter to cross the kitchen and stop the timer. Ty had brought over his lunch plus a lasagna he was supposed to put in the oven…he checked his watch again. Shit…he was supposed to put it in an hour ago. What the hell, he had plenty to keep him busy for another couple of hours.

Popping the casserole into the oven, he set the timer for two hours and ignored the nagging guilt for skipping his exercises again. Maybe he could double up after dinner. If not he could always try to catch up tomorrow. He looked sideways at the activity log and thought about making an entry, but even he couldn't stretch the truth that far. He poured a fresh cup of coffee and moved back to his spot at the table.

When the timer buzzed again, Holden checked his watch to verify that two hours had actually passed. The smell of garlic and tomato were heavy on the air and he wondered how he'd failed to notice the resemblance to a gourmet Italian restaurant. Stiffly he pushed to his feet and absently reached for his crutches, as he blinked to focus his eyes. He hated to acknowledge that it was probably time to buy some of those cheater eyeglasses from the drugstore. After a couple of hours on the laptop, the rest of the room seemed to gather blurry lines.

Stepping toward the kitchen, a sudden searing pain ripped through him as all of his weight came down on his right leg, yet nothing in his foot seemed capable of movement. It felt like a slow motion moment that he should have been able to control: numbness, listing to the right, breath-stealing pain, then crutches flying. His arms flailed, knee collapsed then he was on the ground and his leg was on fire.

"Jesus fucking Christ," Drew said, throwing the door open. He raced across the room, and pushed the crutches out of the way. "Holden…Holden…" Drew was shouting at him, firm hands moving over the back of his head, lightly over his neck, along his shoulders. "Holden…what happened? Did you hit your head? Come on, stay with me. "

The lights in the room dimmed and the edges of his vision started to go black. "Yes," he managed to get out just before the lights went out completely.

*

The first thing he heard was the oven timer. Then he realized someone was calling him an idiot. That felt right, he thought. He was an idiot. He was flat on his back and had no idea why. Blinking rapidly, he saw Drew kneeling over him holding an ampule. Before he could say anything he caught a strong whiff of ammonia.

"Goddammit, Holden. You ass. What the fuck were you doing? Do I have to hire you a fucking nursemaid? Damn stupid selfish son of a bitch. Can't manage to get yourself to your damn physical therapy. Wonder if you even paid attention to what the doctor said you had to do? Do you want to be on crutches the rest of your life?" Drew's voice was tight, his sentences clipped, and Holden realized there was anger mixed with worry.

"Hey, Drew. I'm okay." He started to push himself up, but a firm hand held him down, and Drew leaned over him.

"Motherfucker, how the hell am I ever going to get that dance?"

"If that's your idea of bedside manner, it's a good damn thing you're a vet," Holden said, but he couldn't help the smile that twitched. "Besides, who said I was ever going to dance with you? I'm okay, help me up."

"You sure? Did you hit your head?"

"No, I don't think so." He frowned. "I don't know what I hit. I think...it was slow motion...my foot..." He felt a wave of self-pity threaten.

"Okay. We'll just do a quick check. Unbutton those jeans and I'll help you pull them off. I want a look at your legs. Don't try to sit up yet and let me turn off the damn oven because that buzzer is driving me crazy."

Following orders, Holden unbuttoned his fly, then his hand froze on the last button. Not that he hadn't experienced plenty of undignified moments in the last two months, but damned if any of them had prepared him to be caught going commando while flat on his back in the presence of the man who'd had a featured role in more than one of his fantasies.

"Lift your hips," Drew said, when he returned to kneel next to him. The other man casually undid the last button and pushed at the open waistband. Then his eyes widened, and his light skin took on a definite shade of rose as he slid the jeans from Holden's legs.

Neither man mentioned Holden's nakedness below the waist. Drew's hands were firm as he placed his palms on one thigh and moved downwards, examining each knee in turn. He felt around the joint, flexing and straightening, making sure everything worked. Moving the examination to his calves, Drew kneaded and massaged, first one leg and then the other.

Holden tried every cock-blocking trick he could think of, but nothing seemed to distract his dick from the feel of those warm hands, the brush of calluses against skin, strong fingers pressing in to his muscles. Without looking, he knew he was not only hard but leaking.

Drew moved to settle himself between Holden's legs and lifted a foot into his lap. He tested the ankle joint, then pressed thumbs deeply into the arch, massaging, his touch firm and sensual. When he was finished with the first foot, he placed it in his lap, pressing it against his fly, making Holden aware that he wasn't alone in his enjoyment. Drew lifted Holden's other foot to repeat the examination and massage and they both got harder.

The world was shifting as desire rose, and he felt a primal hunger that had nothing to do with dinner. Need coursed through him, he was a man dying of thirst and Drew was the promise of life. There was a direct connection from the sole of his foot to his cock, and Drew held the end of that line. Surrendering, Holden bit back a moan and put his forearm over his eyes. He couldn't fight his body, couldn't fight against the hands that owned him, couldn't fight his desire for Drew. Climbing higher, he thought he might come just from the foot massage.

"Stop running, Holden. I won't hurt you," Drew said quietly. "Let me—"

Whatever it was Drew was about to say next was lost in the sound of conversation outside their door. Drew grabbed Holden's jeans and draped them over his lap and shifted his position, using his body as a shield. Holden pulled his feet back and placed them on the floor, his knees bent, aching cock covered by the hard scratch of denim seconds before the quick knock on the door was followed by Ty walking in, with Cass trailing close behind.

"Hey, how's the lasagna...oh shit. Uhm...am I interrupting?" He turned back toward the door only to bump into Cass. "Let's go, Cass, they're kind of busy."

Holden met Drew's gaze, silently pleading for discretion. He didn't miss the fleeting look of disappointment, then Drew patted him on the knee, and pushed to his feet. "No, Ty. Holden lost his balance and fell. I was just making sure everything was in working order."

"Shit. Are you okay?" Both Ty and Cass started to rush toward him, he held up a hand to stop them.

"I'm fine. I'm embarrassed enough for one day. How about you guys give me a minute?" When he sat up on his own, Ty and Cass looked to Drew, as if not trusting Holden to tell them the truth.

Drew nodded and waved his hand toward the living room in invitation for the others to move in that direction. "Have a seat. Let me give Holden a quick hand and I'll join you."

Slipping on his jeans as quickly as he could, Holden felt tongue-tied and wished he could explain. Unsure what to say to the man who looked down at him. Once he was buttoned, Drew reached down and pulled him to his feet. He handed him his crutches and waited until they were fastened. Vaguely aware that Cass and Ty were speaking quietly in the other room, Holden struggled to find the right words for Drew. What exactly did you say to a man in these circumstances? What exactly were the circumstances, anyway? Blowjob interruptus? Before he could wrap his brain around a coherent thought, Drew leaned in and pressed a quick kiss to his mouth.

"We're not finished," Drew whispered. Then as if nothing had happened, he called out to the men in the living room. "Who wants a beer?"

****

Drew grabbed three longnecks in one hand and a bottle of water in the other. Then on a second thought, he stopped to rummage through the medicine bottles on the counter until he found the pain medication and got two tablets for Holden. He knew that would likely prevent them from returning to their earlier activity, but Holden was going to hurt from that tumble, whether he realized it or not. Resisting the urge to close his eyes and relive the moment he'd felt Holden's complete surrender, Drew took the drinks into the other room.

First delivering the bottles to Ty and Cass, who sat close together on the love seat, Drew took his own bottle and walked to stand in front of Holden. "Take these," he said, holding out the tablets and the water.

"I don't want—"

"Not a request. Take them or..." Tension hovered between them and he had to bite back a laugh at the pout on the other man's face. Reluctant or not, Holden tossed the pills to the back of his throat before he twisted off the cap and drank deeply. His dick went back into overdrive at the sight of those dark, sculpted lips wrapped around the mouth of the bottle. There was something completely fucking sexy about standing over Holden and watching him do as he'd been told. They locked gazes another long moment, and he let the hunger show on his face before he finally turned away and sat next to him on the couch. Not exactly close enough to touch, but closer than two casual friends usually sat without a reason.

"So, what brings you two over here tonight? Do you want to join us for dinner?" He fought back another smile at Ty's raised eyebrow.

"Actually, that would be nice," Cass said smoothly, obviously aware of the underlying tension in the room. "Unless I'm mistaken, that smell is Ty's excellent lasagna. He's already put dinner out at the main house and left orders for the crew to clean up after themselves. We'd sort of thought you two might want to head to town if you hadn't already started dinner. But, now that I think about it, this is a much better idea."

"Great, we'd love to," Ty chimed in. "Cass, how about you and Holden talk over all your business stuff in here, and Drew and I will set the table. Maybe we could have a dinner free from ranch talk for a change?"

"Doubt it," Cass answered with a laugh.

"Come on, Ty," Drew said, and grabbing his beer from the coffee table, he led the way back into the small kitchen. Not that there was much privacy, since the two rooms ran together, with only a low granite countertop separating them.

"What was that?" Ty hissed, as soon as they were in the kitchen.

The low conversational tones of Cass and Holden from the other room reassured him they wouldn't be overheard.

"It was what the fuck it looked like and your timing sucks."

Ty grinned. "Want us to leave?" he asked as he opened drawers until he found an oven mitt. He pulled out the bubbling, oozing tray of baked lasagna and set it on a folded dish towel.

"God, that looks great, Ty. And no, the moment has passed. Those pills I gave Holden are going to knock him on his ass soon enough. He needs to eat soon to avoid an upset stomach."

"Well, grab the salad, it's in the blue covered container. I brought all this stuff over at lunch, just to make sure he eats. Why he needs to work over here all by himself when we've got the big office—"

Drew laughed, cutting the babbling Ty off mid-sentence. "Have you always been this talkative? Because I sure don't remember that when we first met."

With his hand poised over the silverware drawer, Ty stopped, then turned to look him full in the face. "I'm happy, Drew. There was a time I never thought I'd be this happy, but I am. Cass is a good man." Turning back to finish getting the plates and silverware, he added quietly, "I was in the closet, too, Drew. You can hold the door open for him but don't try to push him through."

*

When dinner was finished, Drew let Ty clear the table, while he walked Holden to his bedroom. "You took quite a tumble today. Your muscles are going to tighten up tonight. Feel up to soaking in the tub?" When Holden stiffened slightly, Drew rested hand on his arm and moved so they were facing each other. He knew Ty was right. There was plenty of heat between the two of them, but unless he was willing to settle for a one-off blowjob, he needed to take it slow. Maybe even romance the other man a little. Definitely needed to let him be comfortable around another man who was interested in being part of a couple. He suspected someone like Holden, a lifelong law enforcement guy in the closet, probably had never had a real relationship before. It was time to change that. He took half a step closer, pleased when Holden didn't back away.

"Holden, I'm not going to do anything tonight except see that you get a good night's rest. A bath will help you feel better, but so will stretching out on the bed. Tomorrow, the next day, next week…we'll get around to talking about what happened this afternoon. And we'll get around to finishing what we started. But not tonight."

Chapter Seven

Tension built in the days that followed the impromptu dinner party. Holden couldn't seem to find his balance, physically or emotionally. His days had become surprisingly busy running background checks for a network of twenty-three ranches in the tri-state area of California, Nevada, and Arizona. Crops were seasonal, the migrant workers came and went, and no one bothered to check on employees who would be around for a month or less. But there were plenty of working horse and cattle ranches and they needed hands that would stick around. Trouble was, cowboys prided themselves on independence. About the only thing they all had in common was driver's licenses and Social Security Numbers. So that was where he started. The ranchers jokingly told him they would cut his salary if he kept losing them good ranch hands after two of the men had turned out to be fugitives. It wasn't exactly top-notch detective work, but he found he enjoyed the routine and the banter.

Locating Juan's cousin was a different problem altogether, and both men knew there was little hope of finding Enrique alive. The coyotes who preyed on those desperate enough to risk an illegal border crossing were unscrupulous and often deadly. His efforts were limited to calling various law enforcement agencies along the southern portion of Arizona and asking questions about human smuggling. Most of the officers he's spoken with recognized his name and offered sincere condolences at his plight. They spoke readily enough until they realized he was no longer Sheriff Titus, but Holden Titus, doing a favor for a friend. Then, the blue wall closed down and he got as much information as any reporter or member of the public would get. Exactly nothing.

The front door to the casita swung open and Holden's next problem walked in looking surprisingly cheerful. "You ready?" Drew called out.

Frowning, he wracked his brain for anything he'd said he would do. A quick glance at the computer's monitor confirmed it was Wednesday, so he hadn't lost completely control of his week. "Ready for what?"

"Your workout. I know you've reduced your visits to twice a week, I assume because of the distance involved, but that doesn't mean you skip the PT. Come on, change your clothes and we'll head over to the workout room in the main house."

"You're a fucking veterinarian, not a physical therapist. Do I look like a goddamn horse?"

"No. More like the horse's ass. Hurry up; I don't have all day. I'll meet you there." And just like that Drew was gone.

Holden contemplated standing the other man up, but he knew the stubborn fool would wait him out. Or worse, tell Ty and the two of them would gang up trying to cheer him out of his bad temper. As if he didn't deserve to be bad-tempered if he wanted.

After changing into a loose pair of shorts and a plain white T-shirt, Holden used his crutches to cross the hard-packed dirt, then entered through the gate and followed the path into the garden that was Cass's secret joy. In addition to the organic vegetable plot, he had several citrus trees and the scent of limes, lemons, and oranges mingled in the hot afternoon air.

When he entered the room Cass designated as a gym, Holden was surprised to see that Drew sat on the vinyl-padded bench, his back to the door, working his laterals on the weight machine. He wore a sweat-soaked, battered grey shirt that stretched tight across his shoulders. Without looking around, Drew spoke around puffs of breath.

"You're supposed to start with the treadmill. Keep it flat and slow. Try not to put too much weight on your hands. I've read the notes, and you should be up to a twenty-minute walk on here daily."

"What the fuck, Van? How did you get my record?"

"Let's just say you're not the only one with some investigative skills." He stopped and turned to face Holden. His face was flushed and sweaty, the smile was warm. Wiping his face with the towel, he said, "Come on, Holden, we both know you have to do this. Let's just skip the argument this time. Walking twenty minutes, leg presses, stretches, whirlpool, and massage. I've got the whole routine. If you want an upper body workout, you can do that tomorrow."

He stared at Drew and the moment stretched out. He thought of and discarded half a dozen arguments, before he gave in and moved with poor grace to the treadmill. Drew didn't say a word, just turned around and went back to his workout, but Holden knew he was watching in the mirror. Attaching the safety strap, he moved onto the conveyor and took a minute to familiarize himself with the controls. The he put the machine on its lowest setting and slowly, painfully forced his feet to take more weight. At the end of twenty minutes, nearly all his weight was resting on his forearms, and the strands of spaghetti masquerading as his legs wouldn't have supported a feather. When the machine glided to a stop, Drew was there to put an arm around his waist and help him from the machine. Determined to finish the workout, Holden straightened his spine and said, "Leg presses."

Bend knees, straighten knees. Ten fucking times. How hard could that be? Sheer determination not to appear weak in front of Drew made him push himself through the last three presses, despite the tightness in his throat, the harsh escape of breath with each bunch and release of muscle.

"Good job," Drew said, wiping his face once again. Holden had lost track of what Drew had been doing, all he'd been able to see was the slide and retreat of the metal plate as his trembling leg muscles pushed the measly ten-pound weight.

Drew passed him a bottle of water, and then went to the corner of the room to wrestle a large folded mat to the empty spot in front of the mirror. "You did good. Let's stretch out those legs before the whirlpool."

Unsure if he could stand, Holden was grateful when Drew reached down to give him a hand. He pushed slowly, painfully to his feet. The men stood toe to toe, chest to chest. Drew was only an inch or two taller, but Holden wasn't used to standing this close to someone and looking up. He moistened his lips, and when Drew's gaze scanned over his face and settled around his mouth, Holden's already quick breath hitched a little in the back of his throat.

Turning to the side, Drew wrapped an arm around Holden's waist and together they moved to the mat. Once again, Drew helped Holden lower himself and this time sat down across from him, legs spread in a vee. "We go nice and slow here. This isn't about how far you can bend or reach. This is strictly to stretch the muscles that you've been working and maybe a few of the ones you've been ignoring."

Together the two men slowly stretched. Holden tried not to focus on the large package in front of his face every time Drew pulled gently on his arms to help him stretch. He had to give Drew credit. There was no added sexual innuendo. This was all about the business of helping Holden heal.

"Right, that's it. Take fifteen minutes in the spa and then come back out here and I'll rub your legs down and you'll be finished for the day."

"Why are you doing this, Drew?"

"Because I can. And because you need somebody to push you. You're going to have to take some responsibility and do this most days by yourself. But I've got the next few days free and I plan to see to it that you get this rehab going. I know how I'd feel if I had to count on Ty to drive me to town and exercise in front of a bunch of people. You're not broken, Holden, but you were hurt. If you don't keep after the rehab, this is the kind of injury you won't recover from. Eventually, your legs will waste and there's no damn reason to let that happen. So for now... you still promise to go to rehab twice a week. Two more days a week, you're stuck with me and this little gym. Anything you want to do above and beyond that is all good. Now go on. I'll be here when you get out."

*

The bathroom that was attached to the gym was surprisingly large. An etched-glass shower stall dominated one corner. Curious, he opened the door to a space large enough for three or four people, with multiple spray heads so that everybody could still get wet. Even those sitting on the tile bench. Closing the door on that fantasy, Holden turned to examine an already filled and slowly churning hot tub, the size he usually associated with backyards and poolsides. The area surrounding the tub was a happy mixture of plants and large palms, all with brightly painted pots, set on uneven and irregular red flagstone pavers. There was a distinctly south-of-the-border patio flavor to this luxury garden spa. Obviously Cass didn't mind spending his money on things that made him feel good.

Leaning against the cool tile walls, Holden tried to maintain his balance on trembling legs, while his fingers fumbled to push his shorts off his hips. Once he was finally naked, he used the edge of the door and safety railings inside the shower stall to support his weight while he rinsed. Turning off the water, he stood naked for a moment, judging the distance between the tub and the cast iron baker's rack stacked with neatly rolled white towels. He contemplated trying the short distance without his crutches, but decided it would be too embarrassing if he slipped and landed bare-assed naked on the floor. Compromising, he used a single crutch to support his weight, the rubber tip bumping on the uneven surface of the floor. Using the handrails, he lowered himself carefully into the hot water, allowing his body to adjust to the heat before turning on the hard, swirling jets. When he was in up to his shoulders he leaned his head back and closed his eyes and thought.

Although the casita was simple enough and contained nothing as luxurious as this bathroom or the home gym, it was still more than he would be able to afford on his own. Once he received his settlement from the county and all his debts were paid, he still had expenses that needed to be covered. There were things in his life that needed to be taken care of, things that people like Cass and Drew would never understand. He didn't know much about the veterinarian's background, but he knew enough to be able to tell he'd come from at least a little money. Holden could not allow himself to get used to living this way.

The luxury was nice, being around all men was nice, but it wasn't something he could do for long. If the job continued to work out, maybe he could work from Laughlin or Needles. He'd have to check the cost of living and other things about those communities.

Lost in thought, he jumped when Drew spoke from behind him. "That's long enough, you don't want to shrivel up like a prune. I'm just gonna rinse off then I'll join you back on the mats. Just wrap a towel around your waist."

Holden tried not to stare while he dried off, then moved past the shower on his way back into the gym. It was pretty damned hard not to notice the acres of creamy white flesh and even harder to resist opening the door for a closer look.

Keeping the towel wrapped firmly around his waist, Holden stretched out on the mat and told his dick to stand down. From now on he would have to come do this on his own because he wasn't sure if he could keep from touching Drew. On the other hand, since he was only going to be at the ranch a little while longer, maybe there wasn't any reason to keep fighting his attraction. After all, he would've given in at that first kiss. He definitely would've given in when they were on the kitchen floor. He wanted Drew and he knew the feeling was mutual. Maybe they should just get it over with…a quick blowjob and a fuck so he could ease the constant itch.

Maybe then he could concentrate on putting his life back to normal. It was already summer and there were decisions that couldn't be put off much longer. That unhappy thought served as a cold shower to his fevered libido.

*

"Ready?" Drew asked, stepping back into the room and breathing in the smell of fresh soap mixed with the sweat from their earlier workout. Holden was lying on his stomach, legs splayed, head resting on his folded arms. The stark white of the towel contrasted sharply with the dark chestnut-brown of his broad back.

"Does my answer matter?" Holden laughed as he answered, and Drew blew out a breath he hadn't been aware of holding.

"Nope, not at all." Drew was cloaked in good intentions and wouldn't back off regardless of Holden's attitude, but he was glad it wasn't going to degenerate into a fight. Not today, anyway. He'd hustled the other man into the gym and so far they'd avoided a direct confrontation about the workout or about how he'd obtained the physical therapy records. It might not last, but he hoped the easy camaraderie of the gym would smooth over any rough spots.

Drew had thought long and oh-so-fucking hard about this massage, and decided he wasn't going to add in any of the sexy stuff from the other day on the floor. This would be a brisk rub of the muscles, a smoothing away of the lactic acid to ease any soreness from the work out. If the only way for him to win Holden's heart was with a slow seduction, then that's what he'd do.

With firm hands and a matter-of-fact attitude, he worked one leg from the ankle upward toward the top of his thigh, then switched to the other leg. He kept a steady stream of conversation, everything from the weather to the Diamondbacks, all casual, all normal. Drew absolutely wasn't going to think about how the velvety skin and firm muscles felt under his hands. He wasn't going to watch the slide of his own tanned hands as he rubbed against Holden's darker, nearly hairless legs. He definitely knew better than to pay attention to the way his thumbs dug deep into Holden's thighs, as he slid his hands up under the towel. This was about healing, not seduction. He hoped his dick was paying attention.

At first, Holden's responses were conversational. When his voice deepened and the answers became one or two whispered words, Drew stopped talking and let Holden drift. It didn't take long before the deep, rhythmic breathing settled in. The muscle fatigue mixed with relaxation put the other man to sleep.

*

Drew spent the afternoon in the kitchen watching Ty put together the meal for the ranch hands. Despite the heat, the men still enjoyed a hot meal most nights.

Tonight's menu was grilled steaks and summer vegetables. After cleaning and cutting summer squash, peppers, and onions, Ty put the veggies in an enormous zip bag to marinate in the refrigerator. "You want a beer?" Ty asked.

"Sure, I'll get them. What are you making now?"

"Brownies. I can make a lot at once with very little effort, but everyone thinks I worked all afternoon. They're Cass's favorite." He kept talking as he moved around the kitchen and gathered what he needed.

Opening both bottles, Drew handed Ty one, then took a long pull from his own. Icy cold carbonation danced over his tongue and cooled the back of his throat. "Hits the spot."

"Yes. So what's happening between you and Holden? Anything?"

"Not high school, Ty."

"Drew...I know you. Asking you to move in there was pushing the boundaries, now I want to know if it worked."

Frowning at his beer bottle, he thought about his answer for minute before speaking. "There's always been something there, you know it as well as I do, Ty. I don't think he's quite as...inexperienced as maybe I thought..."

"That a problem?"

"Hell no. You know me better than that. It's just—Christ, color me a teenage girl." He took another long swallow to finish his beer, then swiped his hand across his mouth. He spoke very quickly, trying to get the embarrassing words out of the way. "I want what you have, okay?"

Ty stared into the bowl, swirling the wooden spoon, and the rich, dark smell of chocolate filled the kitchen. Neither man spoke, the moment stretching as they both seemed to be mesmerized by the work of making brownies. Once the dark batter was poured and the sheet tray placed in the oven, Ty turned to face him.

"I never expected this," Ty said with a little jerk of his head. "It's not what I knew, not what I grew up with. It creates misunderstandings sometimes when you start off in different places, from different backgrounds. If you want this then you're going to have to work for it. Maybe you should make sure Holden wants the same thing before you go too much further. Know what I mean? I don't want to see you get hurt."

Thinking it might already be too late for his heart, Drew returned to the casita, determined to start talking things out with Holden.

*

He heard the crash and splinter of glass as he was opening the front door. "Goddamn motherfucking sonofabitch!"

"Holden? What's wrong? Are you hurt?" Drew rushed inside and found Holden leaning on a crutch in the doorway to his bedroom. He rushed to his side, prepared to help the man to the bed.

"Take your goddamn hands off me." Holden spit the words and pulled away from Drew's grip. He moved stiffly into the bedroom and in one jerky motion managed to sit and throw his crutch across the room narrowly missing Drew's head.

"Hey, what's wrong? Are you okay?" Drew didn't miss seeing the broken glass on the floor near the bathroom door. It looked as if the crutch wasn't the only thing Holden had thrown.

"No, I'm not the fuck okay. I actually have a lead in looking for Juan's cousin down near Sierra Madre, but the ass won't talk with me on the phone."

Still not understanding the problem, Drew remained silent, but retrieved the crutch, then walked over to place it next to the bed so Holden could reach it.

After a long pause, Holden's shoulders slumped, he dropped his head forward, and let out a sigh. "Shit."

Without waiting for an invitation, Drew sat next to Holden. "Want to tell me about it?" Reaching up, he hesitantly brushed his hand over the soft cotton polo shirt. The muscles beneath his hand were rock hard. So much for the spa and massage earlier.

"Yeah. I got this call from an old friend who works for the Border Patrol, but I need to go to this little hole-in-the-wall town way down in southern Arizona—"

"I know where it is. I'm from right near there. So what's the problem?"

"The problem is, Carter wants me there tomorrow night. I just got off the phone with the damn doctor and he won't clear me to drive for another week at least."

Holden was so wound up he either didn't notice or didn't mind as Drew turned his one-handed shoulder rub into a caress. He stroked his fingers along the exposed dark skin just above the collar and wanted to taste. He could smell Holden. Rich, spicy, exotic. Heat poured from him, washed over Drew, pulled him in. He leaned closer and Holden turned to face him, so close now that their breath mingled. "That's not going to be a problem." His voice was a whisper laced with desire. "I'll take you." Then he pulled them together and claimed Holden's mouth.

Chapter Eight

Drew's mouth captured his, a hot searing press of lips that he was helpless to resist. Passion burned between them. One firm hand on the nape of his neck held him in place, while the other cupped his cheek. Their tongues tangled, moans escaped, teeth scraped. Then he was being pushed back onto the bed.

"Holden."

"I don't..." He didn't know what he wanted to say. He wanted Drew. That had never been in question. But he was worried the younger man wanted more than he was prepared to give. More than he *could* give. "Drew...hang on—"

Before he could think how to explain himself, Drew captured his mouth again and he was lost in the kisses. The hard press of Drew's chest over his body, the length of him pressed through the fabric of his shorts. They were both hard and Holden didn't want to stop.

"Just for tonight. We'll talk tomorrow, but tonight? Let's just enjoy each other. No promises, no expectations, just each other. Then tomorrow I'll drive you to Tucson and you can take care of your business." Drew rose up on his knees and pulled his shirt over his head. Never looking away, he unbuttoned his khaki shorts and lowered the zipper. The broad tip of his cock spilled from the opening.

Holden couldn't move, could only watch as Drew moved back far enough to step off the bed and slide his shorts down his thighs, until he stood naked and ready. This could go bad in so many ways, but his mouth watered at the sight of all that beautiful skin just waiting to be tasted. Still he didn't move.

With a small growl in the back of his throat, Drew reached for the waistband of Holden's shorts, and he lifted his hips to give Drew access. Tugging his shirt over his head, he tossed it on the floor to join the pile of hastily discarded clothes.

Drew dropped to his knees and pressed his face to nuzzle against Holden's cock. "God, I want you." Unexpectedly, Drew stood again and crowded Holden, forcing him to climb fully back onto the bed. Then his long, lean frame was pressing down and hip to shoulder they were skin against skin, cock nestling against cock. It felt so good, so right.

Arching against Drew made their cocks drag together, the dusting of hair on Drew's chest scraping against Holden's nipples. Everything was friction and heat, hard muscles, rough scrape of beard, whispered demands.

Holden moved his hands down the tight muscles of Drew's strong back, his fingers moving over each vertebrae, tracing over the muscle, touching the velvet skin, following the length of spine. He slid his hands further down until he found the even tighter muscles of Drew's ass.

"Oh God," Drew moaned. Holden lifted him slightly until he had them cock to cock, sealed together. Drew's weight drove them down against the mattress, Holden's hips lifted them back up. The kisses were hard and wet and dirty as they ground together.

He shifted his hand until his finger found Drew's crease. Drew moaned and pressed even closer against Holden, drawing his knees up, opening himself, inviting Holden to explore.

He kissed Drew or Drew kissed him, he no longer knew which of them was in charge. All he knew was this felt more right than anything ever had before. He pulled back from the kiss to admire the look of the two of them, dark against light, so much more than black and white. The color of their skin, the tight coiled curls of his chest hair, the soft silky strands of Drew's. His own dark nipples against a dusky copper. He wanted to see their cocks together, to hold them in his hand. But he didn't want to pull away, didn't want to lose the friction. He was so close to coming.

"Not going to last much longer, Drew."

"Yes, ready." Then they moved faster, pre-cum adding a bit of slick as they rubbed against each other. Every angle, every brush of skin brought him closer to the edge. He slid a finger between the globes of Drew's tight ass until he found the pucker. When he tapped against Drew's opening, there was an answering flutter of invitation. Oh yes, he wanted that…would have that. But right now he needed release. They both did. Pressing just the tip of his finger inside, he was rewarded by the spill of heat as Drew joined him and they crashed over the edge together.

They lay like that for a long time, hearts racing, breath rapid. Holden knew he should back away, not let either of them become any more involved. Drew was young, had his whole life stretched in from of him, the possibilities endless. Holden had responsibilities that the other man couldn't even begin to imagine, and real life wasn't going to wait much longer.

Ignoring the inner voice that called him the worst kind of hypocrite, he slid his palms along Drew's back and then wrapped him possessively in his arms. Threading his fingers into the silky strands of dark blond hair, he pulled hard enough to raise Drew's head from his shoulder. He had a moment to see Drew's face. The brush of freckles that dusted over his nose and cheeks. The hazel eyes that were flecked with green and gold, and half hidden beneath heavy lids. The wide mouth, always so expressive, ready to burst into a smile, or turn down at the corners when something displeased him. Now those lips were parted and swollen from their kisses. He crushed their mouths together, wanting to mark Drew, wanting to claim him and shout to the world. *Mine.*

Why after all this time had he finally found someone who fit him? And he wondered if it was going to be one heart or two broken in the end.

****

Drew wanted to stay right where he was if it meant Holden would touch him, kiss him like this forever. The big hands smoothed up his back and tangled into his hair, tugging him into a kiss that was different than any they'd shared so far. This time, he was the one claimed with a brutal possessiveness that stole his breath. Then Holden breathed into him, and gave him a new life. He belonged.

The thought shook him to his core. He'd wanted Holden, there was no doubt, wanted a relationship. He'd even gone so far as admitting he'd wanted what he saw between his friends. But this…this was the first time he'd actually understood the depth of feeling possible between two people. There was no other way to describe the shift in his heart at the possessive hug and kiss. Holden was his and he belonged to Holden. Whatever had come before didn't matter because "Home" had a new definition.

When his dick started to pay attention to the new, demanding kisses, Drew pulled back to whisper against Holden's mouth. Despite the message his heart was getting, he needed to hear it, hear Holden say he wanted him for more than a little frot. Wanted him for more than a one-off.

"Holden?"

"Right here, Drew."

"Will you let me stay in here tonight? Sleep with you?"

"Mmm hmm." There was a long pause, and Drew's pulse danced crazily as he waited to hear if he'd read it all wrong. "Not finished with you. Just try and leave."

He smiled against Holden's mouth. Okay, maybe it wasn't a declaration of love, but not finished was good. He was going to make damn sure he was never finished.

"I'll be right back, going to clean up, bring a washcloth." He started to move away, but Holden's grip on the back of his head tightened and pulled his face back down. With a swipe of tongue, Holden demanded entry, and the short, hot kiss made his damn toes curl.

"Hurry back."

As if he'd needed incentive. He nodded, then pushed away, feeling the cooling pool of their mingled cum chill against his skin. Standing still for a moment to let his muscles catch up with his intentions, he looked down at his sticky stomach and fully recovered cock.

Behind him, he heard Holden sit up, then the swipe of a broad hand came down hard on one ass cheek. *Shit.*

"Turn around." Holden's voice was pitched so low that he practically growled the words. When Drew complied, Holden grabbed his ass cheeks, fingers digging in hard enough to leave bruises tomorrow, but damn if he cared. Then those perfect lips wrapped around the head of his dick, and standing became a problem as Holden took him deep and fast.

Gripping Holden's shoulders, Drew pumped his hips, meeting Holden's mouth, pushing into his throat. Holden held on, guiding them both to the pace he wanted. Demanded.

With a loud pop, Holden pulled off. "Help me up. I'm going with you."

They walked together, arms around waists, the awkward gait of lovers refusing to let go made more difficult by Holden's need for support. Drew kept a firm grip, even while he reached in to turn on the water. Not as luxurious as the stall in the main house, this shower was large, with a low, broad bench on the back wall. There were two adjustable nozzles, one mounted on an arm that could be swung around overhead, the other a handheld on a long hose. Shuffling with Holden, he moved him to the bench, keeping his grip firm until he was seated.

"Let me wash off first, then I'll get you," Drew said.

"Not a damned invalid," Holden snapped. Deliberately, Drew turned his back as he sorted through the bottles of soaps, shampoos, and…oh thank heaven…lube.

"No, you're not. I just want to wash you…taste you. Before you fuck me." Without waiting to hear the response, Drew stepped under the spray and washed his hair, then quickly scrubbed the rest of his body. He might have taken a little longer than necessary when he bent at the waist to run the washcloth over his legs. Might have moved back just a little closer to Holden. Might have shivered when fingers brushed against his ass, and he realized Holden was tracing the handprint he'd left behind.

Washing Holden was a study in contrasts, their differences adding an exotic touch to the rich aroma of the coconut scented body wash. Water beaded against the darker skin, shining like jewels that he lapped up, tracing the rivulets of water with his tongue. Holden's long cock was thick and curved back toward his stomach, so dark it was nearly purple. Wrapping his lips around the crown, Drew caught the salty taste of pre-cum and wanted more. Reminding himself to take his time, he explored, running his tongue over Holden's dick, following a trail to the heavy sac, drawing a testicle into his mouth.

"Fuck," Holden muttered, pulling himself from Drew's lips. "Need you, now." Holden reached for the lube, then froze, his hand in midair. "Condom?"

"Not here." Drew said, and felt a flutter deep in his belly. Having a guy's dick two inches from your hole was not the time to make this decision...but he'd known from the first moment he'd laid eyes on the sexy sheriff that what he wanted from him was different. Was more than the careful one night stands, more than the string of boyfriends that never seemed to work out quite right. Any doubts had been brushed away with the possessiveness in the other room.

There were things Holden didn't know, and despite his earlier intentions to keep them secret, Drew now realized he could show Holden just how much he cared. He would tell him what had happened that horrible day, and then ask for the ultimate in trust between lovers. Because that's what they were now, he could feel it in every touch, every kiss. With a mixture of dread and excitement he met the dark look with his own steady gaze. "I was here that day, right after you were...hurt."

Holden's brow creased, and Drew knew he was wondering at the sudden introduction of such an unhappy topic. "I don't remember. I don't remember anything from that afternoon, but I didn't see your name on the witness statements."

"That's because I got there after everything was finished. Cass was hurt, Ty was in and out of some sort of flashback, but you..." He swallowed hard, then continued. "You weren't breathing. I did CPR then worked to control the bleeding until the EMT's got there."

"It was you who saved me? Why didn't anyone tell me?"

"I asked them not to. Holden, don't look away. I wanted you then, I want you now. I was afraid that knowledge might get between us and there already seemed to be too much in our way."

"So why the fuck tell me now?" Holden shifted, as if getting ready to push himself to his feet. Drew couldn't help but notice they both had lost a little of their happy-to-see-you.

"Because we were both tested then. You, because they had to for surgery, me because it's standard when there is ungloved medical contact. We're both clean, Holden, I promise." He tried not to wince at how desperate and trite he sounded. Drew reached for the lube and pressed it into Holden's hand. He turned off the water, opened the plastic curtain, then reached for a towel. Without speaking, he dried himself, wondering what was going on behind those dark eyes. Grabbing another towel, he knelt and began to wipe at the water beading among ripples of gooseflesh on Holden's legs.

"Not an invalid," Holden repeated his statement from earlier. But there was a different quality to his voice, softer, intimate.

"No," Drew agreed. Then the words he'd intended to keep to himself spilled out. "Will you make love with me?" When there was no answer, Drew finally raised his face, resigned to accepting he'd blown it.

Large hands cradled his face and the moment stretched out between them. Then a look passed over Holden's face, one Drew didn't recognize. Holden blew out a long sigh, then nodded. "Yes."

After Holden finished drying they made their slow trip back to the bed. Bracing himself on the mattress, Holden directed Drew to lie on his back and hold his knees. Nerves fluttered in his stomach. "It's been a long time."

Holden didn't answer except to stretch on his stomach and began to press open, wet kisses along the insides of his thighs. His stomach muscles jumped and twitched under the constant pressure of teeth and tongue along the crease of his groin, down the length of his cock, on the firm skin under his balls.

Strong hands separated his cheeks and Drew moaned at the first touch of the slick, hot tongue, against his hole. Drew rocked his hips, seeking more, but Holden gripped him hard to keep him in place. Noises he'd never made in his life escaped as Holden worked his rim, fucking him with his tongue, until he was desperate for friction, for contact. He wanted the burn.

"Now, Holden. Please, oh, God. Want you now." He hadn't thought through the logistics, but Holden seemed to have no trouble pulling himself up Drew's body. He shifted to support his weight on one arm, and then held his other hand palm up. "Lube."

Drew grabbed the bottle where it had landed next to his hip when they'd hit the bed. He squirted a generous amount into Holden's hand and focused on relaxing his muscles. Holden slicked himself, then swiped the rest of the lubricant over Drew's pucker. He slapped his dick against Drew's ass, rubbing, pressing, teasing until Drew thought he might lose his mind. Then the heavy pressure changed, and the fat head of Holden's cock opened him. Gasping for breath, he fought against the involuntary reaction to invasion as his body clamped down and sweat prickled over his scalp then downward. He burned, moaned, ordered himself to relax, and immediately started moving his hips, needing more.

Lowering to his forearms, Holden moved in small increments, despite Drew's urgent demands for more, faster, harder. Holden's whisper was black velvet, rubbing against his desperate need for more. "So tight, Drew. Relax. So hot. Want you. Need you."

Over and over the words came, stroking against Drew's suddenly fragile heart. He thought he'd been prepared for the increased intimacy when he'd suggested that they go bare. He wasn't. As the emotions threatened to overwhelm him, Drew tried to pretend it wasn't a big deal, just a matter of convenience. Only he wasn't built that way. Ever since his first safe sex lecture he'd known he would use protection until he found the one man he would be with forever. Knowing that Holden was bare inside him…would leave a part of himself behind…had forever marked Drew's heart. Embarrassed, he tried to blink away the unexpected sting of tears. When they threatened to spill, he closed his eyes and tried to turn his head. Holden captured Drew's face between his palms, kissing the dampness away.

Then they were flying as Holden powered into him, pounding, grunting with each slap of hips against ass. Drew rocked up to meet him, stroke for stroke, filled with a need he had never known and couldn't have named. Their coming together had all the force and barely restrained violence of a stallion covering his mate. They were teeth and tongue, thrust and withdraw, give and take.

When Holden shifted his weight to change the angle, he brushed against Drew's prostrate and there was no warning, no holding back. He dropped his feet to the bed, back arched, knees falling open. "Gonna…can't…" On the next stroke he lost any ability to speak, as he pushed up hard into the stroke and his ass clamped down. He was gripped by a powerful orgasm that seemed to start in his toes and involve every muscle in his body and wet heat spilled over his stomach.

"Fuck," Holden shouted, as he grabbed Drew's ankles, lifting them, bracing so he could bury his cock as deep in Drew's body as it would go. Holden shuddered, his muscles taut, breath harsh, and Drew felt the spasms as his lover came inside him.

This time when the tears came, Holden rolled him over and cradled him against his chest. "It's okay, Drew. I've got you."

Emotionally and physically exhausted, Drew pressed down against Holden, savoring the feeling of being protected, cherished. He fell into a deep and dreamless sleep, secure in the other man's arms.

Chapter Nine

Holden rested his head against the door of the truck and watched through slitted eyes as Drew drove through the early morning. They'd decided to head south first and stop for breakfast along the way.

He'd awakened alone, and experienced a mild moment of loss before he realized Drew was only in the shower, not actually gone. Then the sound of singing from the bathroom had him smiling at the rumpled sheets, the pillow tossed sideways, bottle of lube still on the mattress where they'd left it. He'd been sure to grab the bottle for their room tonight.

As the memories played over in his head, Holden frowned slightly. He wasn't sure where to put the idea that he'd actually died. Would have stayed dead if Drew hadn't saved him.

The truck slowed and bounced as Drew turned in to a full parking lot outside a light pink stucco building pretending it was adobe. "Ready for breakfast?"

"Yep, and ready for more coffee, too."

"Let your legs hang outside the door for a minute, I'll bring your crutches around." Without waiting for an answer, Drew slid from his seat. Slamming the door on any response, he retrieved the crutches from the back seat of the large truck, then walked around to where Holden sat, dutifully hanging his feet out the door.

"Not an invalid," he said, but the memory of the words made him smile, totally ruining the effect he'd been aiming for.

"I'll say. Of the two of us? I think you may be the one walking most normally this morning."

Flooded with the memory of the pounding he'd given Drew's ass, Holden placed his hand on Drew's arm. "You okay? I didn't hurt you…"

Grinning, Drew said, "Let's just say you're on my mind every time I sit, but I think I'll be just fine if you want to try that again, later. Come on."

With a steadying hand on his waist, Drew helped him down from the big truck and then released him as they made their way inside. A waitress straight out of casting central in Hollywood called over her should for them to sit anywhere. Conversation buzzed but Holden noticed the quieting of each table they passed as they made their way to the only open booth at the far end of the restaurant. This was a local's place, so even though they were on the main traffic route that led to and from Lake Havasu, most travelers would stay to the popular chain restaurants.

When they were settled, their pink-clad waitress bustled over with menus, two mugs, and a pot of coffee.

"Hey, Doc," she said, plunking the down the cups and pouring without asking. "Don't see you out this way much, anymore. I've missed you." Her dark hair was cut at a sharp angle, and she titled her head toward Drew, so the too-black strands brushed against her chin. A pink flush spread up her neck, but it was hard to tell if she was embarrassed or excited. She was certainly happy to see Drew. He seemed oblivious to her turmoil.

"Chelle. No, I don't cover many ranches this far south. We're passing through on the way to Tucson. Thought I'd give my friend a shot at the best breakfast in the state."

"We sure have that here. You want the special?"

"I do. Over medium."

"I haven't forgotten." She winked awkwardly and her smile of straight white teeth was a testament to the miracle of orthodontics. "How about for you?" She spared Holden a quick glance, but kept most of her attention on Drew.

"Well, who am I to argue? I'll have what he's having. Except make mine scrambled."

"You got it. Be right out."

"So, do you have a trail of broken hearts all over this side of the state?"

Drew blinked at him. "What are you talking about?"

"The waitress. What was her name? Chelle? She's got a crush on you." He'd meant it to come out teasing, but he hadn't missed the possessiveness in his tone.

From the quick flash of smile, Drew hadn't missed it either.

Picking up his mug, Drew sat back against the vinyl bench seat and took a long sip of his coffee. "Mmm. She's a kid and I'm not interested. Holden, I'm a gay man. I don't hide that fact. Not from anyone. If you say she has a crush, I believe you, but honestly, I didn't notice."

"When did you know?" Holden hadn't meant to ask, but Drew's casual confidence in who he was and what he wanted intrigued him.

"There wasn't a time I didn't know, I don't think. I mean there was never this big aha moment when I suddenly thought boobs...eewww. My mom never made a big deal out of it, never even asked if I was sure. Just sat me down when I was twelve and explained the facts of life, in her own unique way. When two people are attracted to each other they form a special bond. It was a generic 'they,'" he said, making the air quotes. "They may choose to be intimate. It doesn't matter if the couple is the same sex or opposite sex, the same rules apply. Until you find the right person, the one you love and plan to be with forever, always use protection..." Drew stopped talking and stared at him.

Holden's airway felt constricted, he couldn't look away from the steady gaze of the hazel eyes. What was Drew implying? That somehow by forgoing the condom last night they were now a couple? The low-level buzz of possessive desire that had been stirring in his stomach turned into a full-on roar of approval.

Then the logical part of Holden's brain shouted for attention. He couldn't deny the night was special, but being with a gay man wasn't something he'd be able to do. The moment was finally broken when Chelle returned plunking down more food than any two men could possibly eat. In addition to the eggs, the platters held ham, sausage, bacon, and hash browns.

"Be right back with the pancakes and a refill of the coffee."

"Pancakes, too?" He looked his question at Drew, who was busy cutting the eggs with his fork, and spreading the gooey yellow yolk over the potatoes.

"Best breakfast in the state. Not kidding. Eat."

The rest of the meal passed in relative silence as they stuffed themselves to the point of bursting. Drew dropped a twenty on the table before Holden could reach for his wallet. Then they were back in the truck with cardboard cups in the plastic holder. Soon enough the rural road met up with the Interstate and they were heading west.

Despite his earlier discomfort, the drive was companionable, and at Drew's suggestion, he kicked off his shoes and twisted to stretch his sore legs along the bench seat. Leaning back, he closed his eyes, and Drew's hand resting possessively on his leg felt right.

*

"Wake up, sunshine."

Holden blinked his eyes open, surprised to see they were parked in front of a long, low ranch-style house on a neat street of similar houses. The uniform desert landscaping spoke of a planned community, the size of the yards spoke of money.

"Where…"

"My mom's. I told her we'd stop by on our way through Tucson. Believe me, neither of us wants to see what would have happened if we hadn't stopped for at least a few minutes." Drew looked at his watch. "We're a little early, but don't let on and for God's sake, don't let her bully you into coming back here to spend the night. I've already told her we have a room in Sierra Madre."

Then Drew's door was pulled open, letting in a blast of heat and a warm rich contralto that flowed over them.

"Andrew Van, you get out of that monster truck of yours this minute and give me a hug. Hello, you must be Holden. Pleased to meet you. I'm Rae Van, Drew's mother. Come on, let's not stand out here talking all day. Drew, I really think with all the driving you do you need a more fuel-efficient vehicle. What do you do for a living Holden? Drew is always so mysterious. Do you want to bring in your bags? It seems foolish to spend money on a room when I have two perfectly fine guest rooms…or would you only one want one room?"

Apparently reaching the lung capacity necessary to continue, Rae paused for a breath, leaving that awkward comment hanging out there.

"Mom, good to see you. Now step back and let me give Holden a hand down from the truck, he's got a bit of a leg injury right now. I told you that he works for the ranch, does background investigations. He lives there in one of the casitas. I'm fine. We have a late appointment with someone for his work down in Sierra Madre, so we're going to stay there tonight and head back early in the morning. And I can't drive something smaller because I need the four-wheel drive and extra room in the cab because of my job. You don't want me working in town treating a bunch of over-fluffed Pomeranians, do you?"

Holden laughed out loud, a full out, up from the gut laugh that startled the two Vans who turned to look at him with identical hazel-green eyes. "Well, at least I can see you come by it honestly," Holden said. He pushed himself slowly from the truck while Drew and Rae rushed around to meet him.

Grinning, Rae said, "I'm sorry. You'll have to talk fast if you want to get a word in between us." She laughed and a faint trace of wrinkles turned into laugh lines. This looked to be a woman who was happy with her life. He thought Drew would look much the same in twenty years.

They went inside and Holden contented himself with listening to the two of them banter back and forth, sure he missed some of the finer nuances of family-speak. It was nice to get a peek into Drew's life, to see where he grew up, meet the woman who'd raised him single-handed after his father had been killed when he was only six. He got bits and pieces of family history, along with a heavy dose of liberal politics and tree-hugging philosophy. When it was time to go, Rae sent Drew to retrieve a box of books she said she needed moved from the guest room to the storage space in the garage. Judging from the look Drew sent his way, he was about to be interrogated.

Together, he and Rae walked slowly to the front door, but she seemed to struggle for words for the first time.

"Something you want to ask me, Rae?"

"Actually, I just wanted to welcome you to the family. I know we didn't have much chance to get to know each other yet, but we will. You must be a very good man for Andy to love you."

Drew returned to catch the last part of Rae's words. "Mom, you're pushing. It's not like that."

Rae looked back and forth between them, then focused on her son. "Of course it is, I can see it all over your face." She turned to Holden. "Take care of my boy and you both better plan on being here for at least some of the holidays or I'm coming there to stay with you."

*

After the quiet ride to their hotel in Sierra Madre, Holden had announced he was meeting his friend Chance at the hotel saloon. They hadn't spoken of Rae's words or of what they'd done the night before. They hadn't said much of anything, and Drew had been unsure if it was Holden's way of preparing himself for the meeting or if he was bothered by Rae's words.

Now, Drew sat at the bar and tried to pretend he wasn't staring in the mirror at the two men who sat huddled together at a small table in the darkest corner of the room. Holden appeared to be whispering to Agent Chance Carter, one of the most physically beautiful men Drew had ever seen outside of a magazine. Hair so dark, that in the dim bar lighting it looked black, dark denim blue eyes, and straight, perfect features that looked as if he was a marble sculpture come to life. And oh yeah, he'd sent the gaydar pinging in a big way.

It was Drew's bad luck that the man was a Fed and spoke the same language as Holden. They'd been cozied up for more than an hour, talking, laughing, touching. Oh, nothing too overt, but he'd noticed. Every few minutes, Chance would put his hand on Holden's arm, as if to emphasize a point. Or more likely to offer his ass up on a platter. The growl grew in the back of his throat.

What could he say? He had no claim on Holden. Looking back over the afternoon it was obvious that Holden was uncomfortable. Who could blame him? Drew had pushed with the comment about the condom, then his mother had flat out told Holden her son was in love with him. And wasn't that just a bitch? Because fuck-it-all if she wasn't right. He'd known it was happening, had fought against admitting it even to himself, but it didn't mean he was ready to admit it to Holden. And Holden was definitely not ready to hear it, anyway.

His gaze flicked to the mirror in time to catch Holden throw his head back and laugh. The wonderful full-bellied sound washed over him, even across the crowded bar. His hand gripped his beer bottle.

"Get you another?" the bartender asked, wiping the counter in front of Drew.

"Nope. I think I'm finished for the night." He stood and Holden's gaze immediately met his in the mirror. He was surprised Holden had even been aware of his movement; he'd been so intent in his conversation. Then Holden put his hand on Chance's arm and he turned to face the other man, shutting Drew out completely.

"Ouch. Tough luck, that," the bartender said behind him.

"Yeah, well. Keep the change," he said, tossing a bill on the bar. Then there was nothing to do but go back to the room.

****

"I appreciate your help with this, Chance. I'm actually doing some work for two of the ranches on either side of the Tompkins place. You have my word I'm not going to let on that I received any information." He grinned. "I'll look like a fucking genius."

"Well, you'll look like a genius if these guys are still there. Remember, the federal part of the investigation is more focused on the egress and the main transportation routes. The men you're looking for seem to have slipped through outside the network, so nobody is looking for them right now. Not on this side of the border, anyway. I've given you as much information as I can. I'm sorry for making you come all the way down here, but I can't risk even a hint that I'm talking to anyone about this."

"They won't hear it from me. Remember, I'm just a private citizen, with no official standing and no need to follow legal protocol. If I happen upon some information that might be useful, I'll pass it along to the new local sheriff and he can figure it out from there."

"What about your friend?"

"What friend?" Holden kept his face completely neutral. There was not even the temptation to glance toward the bar since Drew had left several minutes earlier.

"Really? You're going to try that shit with me? If you and the tasty piece at the bar earlier exchanged any hotter looks this whole place would have burned down. And judging from the dirty looks he was shooting us when he left, you've got some groveling to do when you get back to your room."

Grinning, Holden said, "I have no idea what you're talking about. If you saw a good-looking guy at the bar, you should have gone after him yourself. But don't worry. All your secrets are safe with me."

"My mistake. Maybe the bartender has his room number. Because if ever I saw a man who needed a good, hard fuck..."

*

108

Balancing himself against the wall, Holden slipped the key card into the lock, and waited for the green flicker. He pushed inside then quietly eased the door closed. The room was dark, silent. Well, he hadn't exactly planned to get a good night's sleep, at least not yet, but he couldn't deny his body was protesting the last night's activity. His legs had been cramping for the last hour, and he knew he needed to take his medication and stretch out. A bath would have felt good, but he just wasn't up to it. Besides, he had looked forward to snuggling up tight with Drew; he didn't want to wait any longer.

Moving as quietly as he could with the metal crutches, he crossed to sit on the edge of the bed, and leaned the crutches against the wall. He only hesitated a moment before he stripped and crawled beneath the covers. With a bone deep sigh, he stretched out, enjoying the crisp feel of the cotton sheets.

The silence of the room hit him when he finally stopped moving. "Drew?" he said out loud, despite already realizing the room was empty. Struggling to slide across the bed, he pushed to his feet in the narrow space between the bed and the window. Hanging on to the wall for support he parted the curtains in order to peer into the parking lot below. He watched the scene play out, sick to his stomach over what he was seeing. Drew was standing next to his truck, talking with the too good-looking Agent Carter. He saw the flash of a grin, then Chance dropped his arm over Drew's shoulders and led him back into the hotel. Apparently, he was about to give Drew that good, hard fuck. "Shit!"

Using the walls and furniture to support his weight, he made his way to the bathroom and dug out the orange pill bottle. One pill would ease his physical pain. Two wouldn't ease his heart, but they would knock him out. That was the best he could hope for, he supposed. He swallowed the tablets, then slowly made his way back to the empty bed.

*

"Holden?"

Dragging himself from a sleep so deep it was like waking from the dead, Holden tried to get a sense of where he was. Not the hospital...maybe the rehab?

"Holden?" The whispered voice was familiar, tugging at him.

"Drew?" he asked with a mouth that felt like cotton. Apparently he had a brain to match. "Where...what...Chance..." The memories crashed back. Drew had gone back to be with Chance and he'd taken one too many of his pills because he wanted to sleep.

"Holden, you're scaring me a little here. Come on. Wake up. Did you take your pain meds?"

"I don't know, Drew. Did you take it up the ass?"

The lights snapped on and he blinked against the sudden brightness. When his blurry gaze found Drew, all he saw was his back because the man was moving quickly to the bathroom. Pushing himself up against the pillows, he had to bite back the moan that nearly escaped at the pain in his legs. God, he didn't want to admit the doctor had been right about not taking such a long drive.

Drew stepped from the bathroom holding the bottle. "How many of these did you take?"

"I don't need another fucking mother. Why don't you go back to your boyfriend's room and leave me the fuck alone?"

"My boyfriend—"

"Yeah…what? Didn't count on me seeing you, did you? Thought you'd just sneak in a quick fuck with Agent Carter? Let me tell you something Andrew Van. You may have everyone else fooled into thinking you're a nice guy who cares about me… But we both know what's really going on here. You just like to win, right? I pissed you off when I wouldn't dance with you, so you decided to see if you could fucking crush me." He pushed a little higher against the pillows.

"How much did you and Ty bet? Let me guess…you got extra points for bareback? And maybe a little more if you could get me to meet your mother like some goddamn high school date? What was next? One more bonus if I publicly outed myself as your lover? Do you get even more points if I admit I fell in love? You disgust me. Get out. I'll find my own way back."

The color left Drew's cheeks, as if each one of Holden's accusations was a physical blow. "Are you finished?" he asked softly.

Still in the height of his fit of temper, Holden yanked at the sheet, then remembered he was naked. When he shifted his weight to lie back down he was hit with a screaming pain as the muscle in his right calf balled into a tight knot. The cramp stole his breath and he pounded on his leg trying to force the seized muscle to let go. Drew's hands were there in an instant to press his toes back, flexing the joint and causing the muscle to lengthen and loosen.

"Come on, relax, Holden. I've got you. You need to stand up now, walk it off. It will just cramp again if you try to lie down too soon. Let's get you into a hot shower.

"I want you to leave me alone. I can take care of myself." Then as if somehow compelled to do what the other man ordered, Holden grabbed the sheet, twisted it around himself, and moved slowly and painfully to the bathroom. He paused before closing the door. "I want you gone when I come out of here." His voice was just above a harsh whisper as he fought to maintain the last shred of dignity he had left. He closed the door and turned on the water, hot and hard, and tried not to think about what he'd just lost.

Chapter Ten

Drew raked his fingers through his hair as he looked around the room and tried to figure out the best way to fix this for both of them. He needed time get this right, to get Holden to actually listen to what he was waiting to tell him, but the stubborn fool wouldn't be making it easy. It was probably a good thing the ass had gone into the shower rather than stay to fight, because who knew what they'd have ended up saying. Agitated, he paced the room and fought with himself to keep from climbing right into the shower with Holden.

Picking the sheet up from where Holden had tossed it on his way into the bathroom, Drew went to the bed and restored some order to the tossed and tangled covers, replaced the sheet, and put the pillows back at the head. The room was too bright with the bedside lamp on, but too dark with all of the lights out, so he cracked the bi-fold door on the closet to create a little glow without illuminating the entire room. The heavy blackout curtains were partially opened, and he moved to close them, he looked out the window to check on his truck and realized exactly what Holden had seen that set him off. The stupid fool had been watching and seen Chance and him talking in the parking lot. If he'd only been able to hear what they'd actually said...tonight might have gone very differently. With a little space between them, Drew recognized Holden's words for what they were. Hurt and fear.

He was still standing there when he heard the door to the bathroom open.

"What are you still doing here?" The words were hard but the voice was weary. "I told you that I can take care of myself."

"Yeah, you can. But you're not going to." Drew spoke softly, without turning. "I didn't go with Chance, except to have a cup of coffee in the dining room. All we did was talk. He told me not to hurt you." Slowly he turned to face Holden and the breath left his lungs at the magnificence of the man in front of him. Dark skin, broad shoulders, narrow hips wrapped in a tiny hotel towel. Drew crossed to him, relieved when Holden let him pull him close and wrap him in his arms. They stood like that, close, each needing the other yet unable to find the words.

Then Drew remembered the feel of that skin and how much he wanted to taste it, taste Holden. Supporting Holden's weight, he moved them toward the bed, unable, unwilling to let go. Carefully, as if this was his most precious possession, he helped Holden lie back before climbing on the bed to fit himself between the vee of the other man's legs. Much as he'd done that day in the kitchen, Holden closed his eyes and put his forearm up to cover them as if he couldn't bear to watch. A wave of uncertainty washed over him. Maybe Holden couldn't stand the sight of Drew anymore. No...he'd make Holden believe in them.

The glide of palms over hard muscles still warm from the shower made him moan. Last night, he'd only gotten a taste before he'd been pulled off and fucked senseless. He was going to have it now, taste it all, explore every inch of the dark beauty that was so calm below him. He would make him notice, make him beg for it before they were finished.

There was no indifference in the cock he uncovered when he peeled back the scratchy white towel. The thick, heavy cock bobbed, as if thanking Drew for setting it free.

"I don't—"

"Yeah, you do," Drew breathed against Holden's belly, as he spread his fingers wide and rubbed his hands firmly over the six-pack abs. Ignoring the impressive dick wasn't easy, but he wanted to explore, to learn his man. He glided his hands over the soft coils of fine black hair that covered well-defined pecs. Flat nipples darker than chocolate contrasted with the lighter, almost reddish tone of his skin. When he swiped a tongue over one nipple, he felt the jump, the twitch beneath him. The scrape of teeth, pinch of fingers, soothing licks paid off and the reward was a tiny nub that stood to attention. Then he changed sides.

Holden's skin puckered into gooseflesh, but whether from the brush of air conditioning or the fever of his skin, Drew didn't know. Still Holden didn't say a word, wouldn't look at him.

See me.

Moving lower, he explored with his tongue, following the dark path of hair straight to an enticing navel. He dipped in, tasted, then followed further until he buried his face in the smell of Holden, rich, strong, sharp, mixed with the tropical scents of his soap. Drew lifted those poor, tired legs and settled them over his shoulders so he could get at the hidden feast of sensitive skin. Every breath, every touch of his tongue, scrape of teeth made Drew's dick strain against his zipper, but still, his lover held back.

Lifting the heavy sac, Drew licked the tight skin beneath his balls and followed the ridge to his hole. First flat and broad, then tight and pointed, he worked his tongue until he felt the telltale loosening and the man beneath him started to melt into the touch. Shifting again, he flicked at the sensitive skin of Holden's thighs, alternating kisses, licks, nibbles while he unfastened his zipper and one-handedly pushed his jeans down.

When he was clear of his pants, he used both hands to spread Holden wider, to deepen the thrust of his tongue. Holden let out a strangled moan and reached for his cock, but Drew pushed his hand away. "Wait for me, Holden. From now on, you can wait for me."

Raising his head, Holden stared, his lips parted, breath fast. Inspired, Drew slowly licked his fingers as

Holden's gaze settled on his mouth. He closed his eyes when Drew breached his hole with two fingers, but his hips began to rock, even as his hole fluttered.

While one hand worked Holden's ass, the other gripped his cock. Drew gave a teasing kiss to the tip of Holden's shaft, then moistened his lips and slipped the thick curved cock into his mouth. Unintelligible sounds escaped Holden as Drew alternated a rub over Holden's prostrate with a deep swallow and a tight fist stroke. His mouth and hands pressed down, pinning Holden in place, allowing nothing more than little movements, hitches of breath, a long sigh.

"Drew." This voice was no longer the deep, smooth baritone. It was a strangled plea, begging, full of need and want. Drew slid his fingers from Holden's body, and he reached for the lube on the nightstand. When he had them both slicked, he lifted Holden's ass and placed a pillow under the other man's hips.

Never looking away from the dark eyes that burned black with passion, Drew held the base of his cock and pushed the head through the tight ring of muscle. Holden made a half grunt, half growl, and the sound settled somewhere around Drew's balls. He wasn't going to last.

"Move," Holden begged.

Leaning forward, Drew captured his lover's mouth and licked his way inside. When he moved, it was a gentle rocking, an easy push of hips. Slow. Sweet. And the start of forever.

*

Holden thought he understood now why tears had filled Drew's eyes the first time they made love. This was different than any quick fuck. It was personal, intense. Knowing that a part of Drew was still inside him made everything more...intimate. This was real. He shifted his weight and Drew settled more firmly in his arms. His heart swelled a little at the trust, at the hope that filled him. The future. Had it really seemed so bleak only yesterday?

So much had gone so wrong the past two years, and when he'd tried to start over, to get a fresh start? The world had crashed down on him, nearly leaving him dead and making him no longer fit to perform the job he'd counted on to turn his life around. Drew had brought him back to life...in so many ways. Considering his new circumstances, could he make this work? Would he be able to balance everything, bring all the parts of his life together into one perfect fit? He pressed his face against Drew's head and breathed in the scent that was imprinted on his soul. He couldn't give up on this chance at love. There just had to be a way to make everything work.

Chapter Eleven

When they arrived back at the Willow Springs Ranch, Holden was more relaxed than he could remember ever being in his life. They hadn't actually gotten around to saying the words, but their talk of visiting Rae over Christmas, several months away spoke of the future. They brushed hands, sang along with the radio, and with every mile they passed, Holden felt the worries and stress of the last several weeks melt away. They could make this work.

Drew parked in front of their casita and reached over the seat to grab Holden's crutches. He pushed open his door and waited for Drew before he climbed down. He shouldn't have been surprised to see Ty hurrying across the yard to meet them.

Swallowing his own discomfort, knowing Ty would be happy for them, Holden allowed Drew to help him from the cab, then pressed a quick kiss to his lover's forehead before turning to catch the look of surprise on Hardin's face.

"Drew. Holden."

"Hey, Ty," Drew answered. His smile was broad and the hand he placed at the small of Holden's back was possessive.

"Uhm...Holden? You need to come over to the main house, if you could."

"Sure, give us a few minutes to unload, then I'll be right there.

"I got this, you go ahead. I'll join you in a minute." Ty looked as though there might be more he wanted to say, but Holden figured he'd go see what Cass wanted and leave the two younger men to exchange news. No doubt Ty was curious and Drew was bursting to tell him about their trip. Or more accurately, about the new state of their relationship. *Jesus. I'm in a relationship.* The thought made him grin.

Opening the front door, Holden started left toward the office, but voices from the living room stopped him. Backtracking, he turned the other direction, vaguely aware of the front door opening right behind him. Ty and Drew must have followed. Before he had time to turn around, a high piping voice cried out from the other room.

"Daddy!" Then a tiny bundle of dynamite raced to grab him around the waist. "Surprise, Daddy. Did we surprise you? Grandma says we're not staying, but I want to stay. Can I see the horses? I missed you, Daddy."

Every face was turned toward him, watching, waiting. He leaned his weight on one crutch and scooped up his son in the other arm. There was a very quietly murmured oath from behind, but he didn't look back. Instead, his gaze found the eyes of the woman who'd raised him. There was no concern over his injury, no happiness at seeing the son she'd not seen in four months, no joy at the father and son reunion.

Turning his attention to the only important thing in the room, he smiled. "Hey, son, it's good to see you. Of course you're going to stay." He breathed in the scent of his son, and held him tight. When the young boy began to giggle and squirm, he let him slide down his chest to stand in front of him.

"Dad? What are these? Are they like crutches? Are you going to be okay?"

"They are crutches, but I'm going to be fine, son. It's just going to take a little time. I want to show you around, but I need to talk with your grandmother first.

From the look on his mother's face and the fact she'd already told Alex they weren't staying, he knew she'd already figured out the relationship between Cass and Tyler. From the stormy expression on the big cowboy's face, it looked as if June Titus had already shared a few of her opinions. No doubt she had her suspicions about anyone she might have met here and she wouldn't remain silent much longer. His first priority was to take care of his son.

Turning awkwardly, he met Drew's blank expression. *Drew.* They'd been so happy for what was it? Twelve hours? A new record. He should have known he'd fuck this up. He never meant to keep Alex a secret...of course he'd planned to tell Drew. Well, would have if he'd believed they were going to be involved. He'd just never been in this type of a situation. What the hell were the rules when transitioning from a quick fuck to relationship? All he could do now was beg forgiveness with his eyes, and pray Drew would give him a chance to explain later.

Without looking away from the accusation he imagined in his lover's gaze, he said, "Alex, this is my friend, Drew. He's a veterinarian. You know, an animal doctor." Drew raised an eyebrow at the word friend, but didn't say anything. Holden continued. "Drew, this is my son, Alex. Would you do me a favor and take him to the barn to see the horses? Please." He added the last word and hoped Drew knew how much he needed his support at this moment.

After only the slightest of pauses, Drew smiled and squatted in place. He held out a hand and the big grip swallowed Alex's tiny hand. "Nice to meet you, Alex. Would you like to go see the barn and meet some of the horses?"

Alex solemnly shook Drew's hand, then his gaze shot to his father then back to Drew. "Nice to meet you, sir. Do I have to call you Doctor?"

Laughing Drew stood, keeping Alex's hand in his. "Not if I don't have to call you Mr. Titus. You call me Drew. Come on. There's a brand new litter of kittens in the barn, too." Their voices faded as they walked hand-in-hand to the front door.

"How dare you?" His mother hissed. "I did not raise that boy to be sent off with one of your perverted friends."

Ty moved to stand next to him and Cass opened his mouth, but Holden held up a hand. "First of all, you did not raise that boy, I did. He is my son, and had it not been for my unfortunate accident, I would have already brought him to Kingman to live with me. And by the way, thank you for asking. Yes, I'm going to be fine. Second, neither Drew nor anyone else on this ranch is a pervert, and you will be civil."

"Don't you speak to me like that. I can see it was a mistake to come here."

Sighing, Holden tried to maintain control of the conversation, but his mother was a master manipulator. There would be a reason she'd come here to the ranch without warning, and he had a sick suspicion he knew what that reason was. When he'd spoken to her on the phone last week, they'd agreed she would keep Alex for two more weeks while Holden figured out his new arrangements. Obviously since he was no longer sheriff, he wasn't tied to starting Alex in school in Kingman in the fall. He'd planned to check out the other cities in the tri-state area after talking with Cass about making the job arrangement they had more permanent. Knowing his mother and the triumphant look on her face, she'd decided the odds for her scheme had just shifted in her favor. The only thing Holden could think she wanted was custody of Alex. She wasn't going to get it.

"Mother, why are you here?" he asked on an exasperated sigh.

Her eyes narrowed and her voice took on a singsong, wheedling tone. "Why, Holden Titus, how can you ask such a question of your mother? Of course I'm here to see that my only son isn't too badly hurt. But now that I see the…situation…" Her mouth made a little moue of distaste. "Well, I can hardly leave Alex with you. Given you're now unemployed, the only solution is for me to take the two of you to my house, where I can be assured that Alex is properly cared for."

"At least it didn't take us long to get to the point this time. I'm not going back with you. And now that Alex is here, he'll be staying, as well." He didn't bother to look at Cass. The rancher's generosity had been proven time and again. He had no doubt his friend would allow Alex to stay until Holden could make arrangements for his own place.

"You can't seriously expect me to leave my only grandchild out here in the wilderness with these…these…"

"I suggest you stop right there, Mrs. Titus," Cass said in his deep, gravelly voice. "Now I'll only say this once. The nearest hotel is another hour and a half drive from here. You can put yourself back in that car and drive, or you can figure out how to keep a civil tongue in your mouth, and stay here through the weekend. I won't presume to tell you how to live your life, but I'll be damned if you're going to sit in my home and insult me or any of my men, including my partner. For the record, Holden is not unemployed, and he is not without resources. This is his home and we provide all the family he needs, so I suggest you consider that before you make another threat against my friend."

Cass stood abruptly and moved toward the doorway. He paused to lay a hand on Holden's shoulder, his voice soft enough that Holden knew his mother wouldn't hear the words. "I'm sorry, Holden. I overstepped my boundaries, but I cannot standby and say nothing. I'll give you some privacy to talk things through. I meant what I said, though…the insults stop. June may have a guest room here in the main house through the weekend. You do have a job, Holden, and if you'd like to discuss a longer contract there is no difficulty whatsoever. The casita is yours to do with as you like. You and Alex…you and *whomever* you choose may stay there as long as you want." Cass squeezed his shoulder. "Come on, Ty. Let's go find what Drew is getting up to with our newest ranch hand, master Alex." Holding out his hand, Cass tucked Tyler's hand in his, and the two of them walked from the room, much as Drew and Alex had only minutes before.

Turning to face his mother, Holden noticed how stiff and unbending she was holding herself. Despite driving nearly seven hours to the ranch from her Southern California home, she'd made no concession to the heat. Her navy blue suit with the white piping was crumpled around her lap, and her lightly streaked black hair was shellacked to withstand the desert winds. Not an old woman by anyone's standards, yet the pinched mouth and disapproving glare added years to her appearance. Unused to being on the receiving end of anyone's chastising, let alone a gay man's, Holden was sure she wouldn't stay here. Especially since Cass had warned her about speaking her mind. However, June Titus never admitted defeat, he needed to be prepared to deal with whatever was in her arsenal when she returned. Without a doubt she expected to claim Alex at a minimum, and her son, too, if she could find a way. June Titus couldn't conceive of failure.

"I don't believe any further conversation with you would be productive at this time. Just know that I will not allow you to corrupt that young man's mind. I will return for him Sunday noon. Since you are hardly in a position to offer him better than the stable home he has come to count on…without you for the last six months, I might add, I suggest you have him ready to go. It would be in everyone's best interest if you were also ready to leave at that time."

With that ominous pronouncement, she swept from the house to drive on to Kingman, he presumed.

****

Drew wanted to rage. He wanted to scream and yell and throw the ultimate of tantrums. Except he really didn't do scenes and the small hand squeezing his had already started squeezing his heart. Looking down was like looking at a miniaturized version of Holden. The same dark skin with overtones of chestnut, short-cropped black hair that left him wanting to rub the boy's head. Big, dark eyes that tried to see everything at once.

"You live here?"

"I sure do. Sounds like you might be staying here, too."

The expressive mouth turned down at the corners and Drew didn't miss the furtive glance over his shoulder, as if his grandmother might overhear what he was going to stay. "Grandma said we can't...that this was a 'bomination or something like that."

Drew saw the boy's mouth continue to work around the word, trying figure out the meaning from his grandmother's words. "A-bom-in-a-tion," he said, sounding the syllables out for Alex. "It means there's something about the ranch she doesn't like. Let's let your Dad take care of that, okay?"

"She says Mr. Cass and Mr. Ty are gay. That means they like each other, right? My friend's moms are gay, too."

"Yep, that's what it means." He agreed easily. The words were tossed out with a shrug and childish innocence and zero malice. Still, if that was how Holden had been raised, it was no wonder he stayed closeted.

"Hey! Who's this?" called a friendly voice. He looked up to see the blond-haired, blue-eyed Chad bouncing toward them from the casita he was rehabbing. *From my casita.* He'd been looking forward to sleeping with Holden tonight as a lover, in their own bed, and waking up with a morning blowjob, much as they had this morning. The reminder that their living arrangement was only temporary hurt nearly as much as the secret son now walking beside him.

"I'm Alexander Titus," the boy answered in his polite and formal tone.

"Well, it's nice to meet you, Alex. I'm Chad. Is it okay to call you Alex? Are you going to stay here at the ranch with us?"

"Yes, sir. At least, I think so. You're dusty." He said the words in an awed voice, as if grown-ups weren't allowed to be dirty. Given the state of his pressed jeans and button down shirt, Drew wondered if the cast iron biddy ever let the boy play? What the hell was Holden thinking of, leaving his son in the care of the stiff old woman?

Chad laughed. "I *am* dusty. I'm working on fixing up the house so—" he broke off and glanced at Drew, then back to Alex. "So someone can live there. Hmm…I sure could use some help. You look old enough…maybe you can help me paint tomorrow. Do you like to paint?"

"Oh, I think so. I'm four and a half, but I turn five in December. Is that old enough to help?" he asked. Without waiting for an answer he asked, "Do you want to come with us? Drew's going to show me the horses." Alex's thin voice quivered with excitement.

"I'd like to, but I need to finish what I'm doing if we're going to start painting tomorrow. High-fives bud," he said and held up a palm. Alex jumped, slapping their hands together with a nice roll of little boy laughter spilling out.

The barn was easily the largest structure at the ranch, tall with a doorway wide enough to drive a fully loaded truck inside. The inside was clean as far as barns went. Good barns usually were. The men on the Willow Springs mucked stalls and swept the floors daily. Large fans turned lazily, keeping the air circulating in the dark interior. Still, he knew it might be intimidating to a small, city-raised boy, and Drew was unsurprised when Alex's small hand slid into his. Drew reached down and lifted the boy onto his hip.

"This is Candy," he said, walking to the first stall. "She's probably the only horse inside right now. She strained a muscle in her leg the other day, so we've been keeping her a little quiet for a few days to give her a chance to heal."

"Kind of like my dad, right? I mean, he's going to be all right, isn't he?" The worry he hadn't shown earlier at his father's condition showed plain on his expressive face. Drew thought the dim interior and being held might have encouraged the question.

"Yeah. Don't worry, little man, your dad is going to be fine. He just needs rest, a little exercise, and someone to take care of him. Just like this mare, here. When she's better, you'll be able to go for a ride. She loves boys like you."

Candy turned and made her way to the stall half-door.

"Hey there, sweetheart," he said as she leaned over and huffed a hot breath on his hand. He shifted Alex more securely on his hip and reached for the ever-present peppermint treats he kept in his pocket. He unwrapped it one-handed, a skill he'd long since perfected, then held out the candy for the gentle horse.

Alex giggled as Candy's horsey lips captured the mint, then asked, "What's a mare?"

"A girl horse."

Alex squirmed a little as he turned in Drew's arms. "How can you tell she's a girl?"

"Hmm…that's a good question. One way you can tell Candy's a girl horse is because she's a mom. She has a baby almost as old as you are."

Twisting back around, Alex looked at him for a long moment from eyes just like Holden's. Then he turned back to Candy and said very quietly, "My mom died."

Pain sliced through his heart at the quiet words. For Alex, for Holden. Maybe even a little for himself. He'd imagined he was something special in Holden's life, that once-in-a-lifetime chance for a real relationship. Shit. He'd written a damn fairytale complete with happy ending and he hadn't known the first thing about the other man.

Holden had a wife he'd loved enough to marry and have a child with. An important career. A family. While Drew had been busy sharing parts of his life, his childhood home, his own mother, he hadn't been paying enough attention to what Holden's lack of sharing might mean. He'd assumed Holden's reticence was because he was in the closet, but hell, it was far more likely Holden was just a man who had sex with men. Which made Drew nothing but a piece of ass Holden could have on the fucking down-low.

Pushing away his own pain, Drew hugged Alex close. "I'm sorry about your mom."

With the resilience of youth, Alex said, "That's okay. Can I see the kittens?"

A shadow fell across them from the open barn door and Drew turned. Alex exploded from his arms and ran to his father. "Dad...Dad... This is Candy. Drew says I can ride her when she's better. And Chad says I can help paint. I like it here. Can we stay? Huh? Can we?"

Holden's smile was all for his son, as he looked down at the little boy. "Let's go look at the house. Grandma left a little bag of clothes for you. Do you have any shorts? It's way too hot for jeans." The two Titus men turned and left the barn, leaving Drew standing there feeling more lonely than he'd ever felt in his life.

After a few moments he heard the quick pound of sneakers on dirt and Alex raced back into the barn to grab his hand. "Come on, Drew. Dad's waiting."

****

Holden moved straight to the kitchen to get a cold drink and look through the freezer for some ground beef. He removed two soda bottles and held them in the air to catch Drew's eyes. At the other man's nod, he popped the tops on both bottles.

"Spaghetti okay with you, Tiger?"

"Yes," Alex shouted, with a little fist pump. "My dad makes the best spaghetti. Where's my room?"

"Oh, hey. There's only two bedrooms. I think my stuff is probably in your room," Drew said. Holden met his gaze, but couldn't find the words he wanted to say. It didn't matter, because Alex got there first.

"Cool! You live with us? We can share a room if you want. Or do you want to share with Dad? I go to bed at eight. What's your bedtime?" Then he was dragging Drew to the back of the casita, exploring the bedrooms, his happy chatter carrying through the house. *Dear God.*

There had been only a few minutes for a quick conversation with Cass once his mother had left. He could put aside his concerns about a job. That at least was secure for now, regardless of where he chose to live. But he had Alex to think of. And Drew. They'd not even had a real chance together. He didn't know what he'd been thinking last night. He could blame the drugs. Well, and the sex. Drew *had* fucked him senseless.

Shifting his weight between counter and crutch, Holden busied himself with browning the ground beef and chopping the veggies. He paused frequently to drink deeply from his soda, and wished it was something stronger. He needed some time to talk with Drew, time alone so he could explain about Karen, about Alex. And so he could apologize. As if it could make a difference. A young man like Drew wouldn't want to be saddled with a kid.

"Dad, make him stay," Alex wailed, running back into the kitchen.

Drew sauntered back in, the strap to his duffle slung over his shoulder. Holden's heart beat uncomfortably in his chest, and the soda he'd swallowed threatened to come back on him. *Not yet.* They hadn't talked…he hadn't gotten a chance to explain. Then the true reality hit. It didn't matter what he said. He was a father first. He'd held that information back from Drew and led him to believe there could more than just a good time between them. Let himself believe it, too, for a few hours. Now it was time to put his life in order.

"Alex, be polite. Drew will be around. Won't you?" he asked.

Drew looked at him for a long moment without answering. The pain he'd masked earlier with a carefully blank face was evident now. Holden wanted to go to him, to hold him and beg forgiveness. But he couldn't do that. Not right now. Drew squatted down on his haunches to speak face to face with Alex. "I'll be back, little man. I've got some things I need to take care of. And remember, you can help Chad paint the casita next door so it will be ready for me when I get back, okay? We'll be neighbors. At least for a little while."

Slipping the bag from his shoulder, he handed it to Alex. "Can you do me a favor and take this out to my truck? I want to tell your dad something before I go."

Alex straightened his shoulders, clearly pleased to be asked. He half carried and half dragged the duffle out the door.

Frozen in place, watching his son and the man he now realized he'd grown to love, Holden was hit with a wave of grief. How could you mourn what you'd been afraid to dream? He held himself stiffly, rooted to the spot as Drew stood and walked to the kitchen.

"Drew, I—"

"Don't. Holden, can you tell me that you love me? That there is any possibility that you would live with me as a couple?"

Holden's brain froze, his tongue stuck to the roof of his mouth, and he nearly strangled on the words he wanted to say. He knew his mother wasn't done with him. With Alex. If she got even a whiff of his involvement with another man, that he might want to live permanently as part of a gay couple...she'd never quit until she took his son. But how could he explain it to Drew? It would only make the younger man determined to fight for something they couldn't have. Holden wouldn't risk his son. Not even for love.

He dropped his gaze.

Drew nodded, as if that was what he'd expected. "I love you, Holden, but I won't live in your closet. I'll see you around."

Then the light in his life walked out the door.

Chapter Twelve

The next morning, Holden remained at the dining room table in the main house with Cass and Ty, while a wide-eyed Alex went with Juan and the other hands to feed the horses.

"So you just let him walk out?" Ty hissed as soon as the men left the dining room.

"Ty, he was asking me to choose. I can't...I won't risk my son."

"And that's another thing. How come we didn't know you had a son?"

"For God's sake Tyler. When was I supposed to tell you? When I was dying in your kitchen?"

"No asshole. How about when you woke up in the hospital? Or in the rehab? Or fuck, I don't know. Maybe when you moved in here?" His voice dripped with sarcasm.

"I thought I was only staying here for a few weeks. Jesus Christ, everything I've done has been for my son. I've thought about nothing else for the past year and a half and it all blew up in my face anyway. Why the hell else do you think I moved to Kingman?" Setting his coffee cup on the table, Holden balled his fists in his lap to try to hide the shaking.

"I don't know. Why don't you tell us? Wouldn't that be a fucking change?" Ty's cheeks were flushed and there was nothing easy about the set of his jaw.

"Let it go, baby." Cass's tone was mild, but Holden thought he saw sympathy in the rancher's face. "Holden, how can we help?"

Inhaling deeply then blowing out his breath, as if he could exhale the memories, Holden shook his head. "No. Cass, Ty's right. I owe you an explanation." No one spoke, while Holden gathered his thoughts, tried to sort through what was and wasn't important.

"I am thirty-six years old and the only child of June Titus. There was no factor that weighed more heavily in my life until recently. My mother was unwed and only fifteen when she had me. Believe me, there is no one who can dish the guilt any better. I don't know who my father is, but there wasn't a day that went by I didn't hear about him, my mother's sacrifices, or about the importance of creating a new family legacy. It became my role to make up for every real or imagined slight my mother ever suffered. That meant college, a respectable job, and a wife and children. In that order.

"There were a lot of lean years, we practically grew up together in a lot of ways. She worked as a maid at this tiny motel in one of the oldest sections of Hollywood. She never told me how we ended up there, but the owner was this guy old enough to be her grandfather and he gave us a small, un-rentable room in exchange for working as a maid. We lived there on handouts and charity for a lot of years. Then the old guy up and dies and leaves the place to my mother. She'd had more than enough of the hotel business by then and the land was worth a fortune so she sold it and we moved to Orange County."

Cass put his hand over Ty's when he leaned forward as if to ask a question. With a sigh, he leaned back against Cass, so Holden continued.

"Everything became about hiding our past, putting on pretensions. She wanted me to go to law school, fought with me when she realized I wasn't ever going to be the attorney she'd dreamed of. She wanted the prestige, but the job would have killed me. I wanted to be a cop. She didn't speak to me while I was in the training academy, but she was there when I graduated at the top of my class. Then everything became about taking the test for detective and getting married to give her grandbabies.

Needing to do something, Holden levered himself from his seat, stepped closer to the sideboard and refilled his cup from the giant urn of coffee. He set his cup on the table, but remained standing, resting his forearms on the back of the chair, fingers laced together. "Karen was in the academy with me...she was a legacy admission, third generation. She understood trying to live up to family expectations.

"We got on well, liked each other a lot, even dated a few times. Then about six months after we graduated, she came to me in tears. She'd gotten pregnant. She didn't believe in abortion but she couldn't tell her parents. I don't know, it just seemed to make sense at the time that we go ahead and get married."

"But Alex…" Ty started.

Holden smiled and shook his head. "No, Alex is all mine. Looks just like me when I was his age. Karen lost that first baby, but we stayed married. We really were good friends and it was easy to be together. It made our families happy, too. Sex wasn't a problem for either of us and we both wanted kids. After several years, she finally got pregnant again."

"Did she know you were gay?" Tyler asked.

"Hell, *I* didn't know I was gay or even bi. I'd been with a few guys in college, but that was just men fucking around on the down-low. A lot of guys did that—it didn't mean anything.

"Anyway, Karen and I were happy enough. Then her mom found out she had breast cancer that had already metastasized. It was quick. Maybe four months from the diagnosis to her death. It took it out of Karen, you know? She took a leave of absence from the department to stay home and care for her mom and I started taking Alex to my mother's more and more.

He blew out a breath. "I should have been paying more attention. I was working double shifts trying to make ends meet. Karen was spending every day and most nights at her dad's, trying to help him cope. Alex's second birthday was coming up and my mother wanted to throw him a small party. It had been weeks since the funeral and she thought it was time to celebrate something.

"Since neither of us had been around much, I pressured Karen into coming to the party. She sat there hollow-eyed, unsmiling. I don't think she even spoke to Alex. She left before the birthday cake and presents."

Rubbing his face as if he could erase the memory, Holden closed his eyes and continued. "I took the next day off work, determined to go to her dad's and bring her home, get her some help. Instead, I found the two of them. Murder-suicide."

He never saw him move, but somehow, Cass was just there, an arm around his waist, helping him back to his chair. Once he sat, Cass kept a hand on Holden's shoulder, as if anchoring him in place.

"You don't have to tell us anymore."

"Let me just get this out. It won't take long. I moved back in with my mother so I had someone to help with Alex, but my own mortality was staring me in the face. I'd moved up through the ranks over the years, it seemed like a good idea to look for another position, someplace a little quieter, with less overtime and a lot less potential for injury. I applied at small cities throughout the southwest, and ended up here. My plan was to get settled and bring Alex over before school in August. That's it—the whole story. I wasn't deliberately trying to hide anything…I just didn't think I needed to talk about it."

"What about the gay-thing?"

He should have known Ty wouldn't let that go. Closing his eyes briefly, he looked for any answer that would make what he'd done to Drew okay.

"No, it's all right, Cass," he said before the other man could protest. "I get it. Drew is his friend. After Karen…it seemed easier to go back to the man on man sex scene. I don't know if you ever ran into it, Ty, but I'd bet it was prevalent in the Navy. Guys who have sex with other men, but who don't identify as gay. It's widespread in communities where being real macho is important." He took a big swallow of coffee, risked a look at Ty's face. Tyler stared back, waiting.

"I'm pretty self-aware. I noticed that I was a lot more turned on by the guys than by any women I met. I went to that club in Laughlin to test the waters, to see if maybe I hadn't been in some sort of denial all these years. Then I ran into Drew. Believe me, I'd already noticed him more than I'd wanted to. You know the rest."

"Do you love him?"

This time Cass did get the first word. "Jesus, Ty. What is this? Their business. Not ours."

"Ty—" His phone rang, and Holden glanced briefly at the unfamiliar number. *Not Drew.*

"Titus."

"I assume you recognize my voice. This is a disposable phone, but let's keep names out of it. I wanted to give you a head's up. That name I gave you the other night is confirmed. Nothing is going to happen on this end for days, because that's still an offshoot. If there's any chance, you're probably it."

*

140

It was funny how life could change in an instant. One minute, Ty had been ready to ream him a new asshole for hurting his friend, the next, the former Navy SEAL had taken over and they'd been planning a covert operation. Not that they had a team or any official standing. But that didn't seem to bother Ty any more than it had bothered him.

Now, he sat in a darkened truck and waited for Ty to return from his reconnaissance of the concrete outbuilding located on a ranch in the remote eastern part of the county. He was pretty sure Ty was the only one having any fun. His replacement, Sheriff Morgan was royally pissed because all he'd been told was to have deputies standing by, and a general location, but not why. Cass was pissed because Ty was on this mission without him while he stayed home watching Alex. Holden wasn't exactly pleased himself, since he was left sitting here in the dark, monitoring the communications Ty had rigged.

According to the plan, Ty would confirm the presence of the illegal aliens, and specifically Enrique, if he could. Then he'd return to the truck and as soon as they were back on the Interstate, Holden would call Sheriff Morgan and anonymously report that Mexican citizens were being held against their will on the Long T Ranch. Juan's cousin would be arrested, but eventually he'd make it home alive.

The radio crackled to life. "Start the engine, we're coming. Fuck...fuck, start the engine. Hurry, they're right behind me."

Dragging himself to the driver's side, Holden did as directed. He had no idea what was happening, but if Ty said hurry, he wouldn't be kidding. Starting the engine, he put the big truck in gear and waited, straining to see against the dark night. The brake lights had been covered as soon as they'd left the main road, and he kept the headlights off. The truck was as invisible as they could make it, but he trusted Ty knew how to find him in the dark.

There was an impact as something thudded into the bed of the truck, followed closely by another truck-shaking thud. Then Ty was pounding on the metal bed, shouting, "Drive, drive."

Ignoring the pain that shot through his leg, he pressed his foot to the accelerator. It was only a muscle and muscles healed—but if some stray bullet hit one of them, they'd be in a lot more trouble than he was prepared to handle. He needed to get Ty and...he flashed a glance over his shoulder...whoever Ty brought with him, out of here.

Great. Now he'd probably be arrested for human smuggling. Gripping the wheel, he focused on maintaining control as the truck bounced and rocked over the desert landscape. When he saw the flat black ribbon in the distance that signified the road, he wanted to accelerate, but it wasn't until the rear window of the truck exploded into a million tiny glass pebbles, that Holden flipped on the headlights and pressed the pedal to the floor. They obviously were not running in stealth mode any longer. He might be lighting himself up like a Christmas tree, but he could at least see the damn way clear of boulders and saguaros. Crouched as low as he could in his seat, he let the big truck loose and with a growl of the powerful engine he muscled them to the highway and toward the relative safety provided by others. He didn't breathe any easier until he saw the headlights of the vehicle that had been chasing them turn back toward the desert rather than follow them onto the main roadway.

He went another two miles just to be sure, then pulled into the emergency access lane. He just sat for a moment, trying to catch his breath, making an inventory of his body parts.

"Whoo-hoo," Ty said, jerking the door to the truck open. The words might have sounded casual, but there was an air of all-business around the younger man. "I got Enrique. You okay, Holden?"

"Yeah." It was all he could manage for a minute, as visions of his son flashed through his mind. "You brought him out. How can I direct the officers to the property now?"

"Hurry and call it in right now. There are three others still there. I could only manage to get one loose. My bad luck they had a sentry posted and he stepped around for a smoke."

Pressing the speed dial button, he watched and half listened as Ty turned to the other man who climbed out of the truck. In rapid Spanish, Tyler rolled off some directions too fast for Holden to follow, but Enrique seemed to understand. They peeled off the plastic garbage bags Ty had taped to the taillights, then

Enrique climbed into the back seat and Tyler nudged Holden to scoot over.

"Morgan? Titus, here. You and your men need to hurry to the Long T. They are already alerted that their security has been breached. Three men are being held against their will in a concrete outbuilding approximately one quarter mile from the main house." He relayed the GPS coordinates, evaded a few questions, then ended the call.

Then they were back riding smoothly along the highway, heading west toward home. He could almost make himself believe nothing had happened. Except for the rush of wind from where a shotgun blast had come too close to his head for damned comfort. Goddamn...*Goddamn it!*

Despite the planning, despite the reassurances, Ty had put them all at risk by attempting a rescue they weren't equipped to handle. Yet, in this moment of brutal honesty, he knew without a doubt, had he been the one to go in, he would have been unable to leave Juan's cousin or anyone else behind. Closing his eyes, he swallowed down the bile and fought against his anger.

Denial had no place here. Had he been whole and healthy...this would have been his job. Even now, he would be the one racing into the scene, weapon drawn, no room in the moment for outside distractions. Thoughts of his son, creating a stable home, their future...those would have been necessarily pushed aside. Time and time again he would have put his Kevlar vest on, buttoned his uniform shirt, strapped on his service belt, and gone to work as if it were nothing more than a routine job. It was exactly what he *had* done.

Reality pressed down, crushing him under the weight of his responsibility. How...why had he thought he could continue to be a cop once Karen died? By the grace of providence he'd been given a second chance to show that his son really was his top priority. He wasn't going to fuck it up again.

Chapter Thirteen

The door to the ranch house opened with a bang. "Ty? Cass? Where is everybody?"

"We're back here, Drew," Cass called. Drew kicked off his boots and headed toward the living room. Cass was stretched out against the arm of the long sofa, his arm around the reclining Ty's shoulders.

Picking up the remote, Ty pressed mute on the Diamondbacks baseball game they'd been watching. "Hey, Drew. Welcome back. Where've you been all week?" Ty asked.

Drew could tell his friend was pissed but playing it cool. He couldn't blame him. After his showdown with Holden he'd taken off without a word to anyone. For the first two days of his self-imposed isolation, he told himself that ignoring Ty's calls was a matter of self-preservation. He hadn't wanted to talk to his friend, hadn't been ready to hear about Holden. It had been a relief when the calls stopped coming. Then his mother had weighed in and called him a coward and told him a few things about being a single parent that he'd never considered. It had taken him another two days to sort through his feelings, and realize that the world didn't actually revolve around him and what he would...or would not tolerate.

None of that mattered now, except for how much groveling he would have to do to get into everyone's good graces again. Since the lights were off in the casita and on in the main house, he figured he could apologize to everyone all at once, then go home. If Holden would have him. If not, he'd wait until the other man was ready. He stood awkwardly, half expecting to be invited to sit. After a moment, he answered Ty's question.

"Hey guys. Sorry. I went to visit my mom. I needed some space...and...I know I owe you an apology and this doesn't cut it, but I need.... Where's Holden?"

"Gone." Ty's one-word answer pierced his heart.

"Gone?"

"Gone. Anything else we can do for you? Because otherwise, we'll get back to watching the game."

Drew looked from Ty's hard features to Cass's more neutral expression, but the tight lines around his mouth showed his anger. Fighting to stay calm, Drew asked the only question he could think of. "Why?"

"What the fuck, *Andrew*? The man's whole life was falling apart and you picked that minute to demand he come out and play by your rules? Or what, you'd walk away without looking back? Fuck you." Ty pushed to his feet, hands clenched into fists, his breath escaping in harsh, choppy bursts. Drew took an involuntary step back, even as Cass stood and took his lover's face in his hands.

"Ty. Ty baby, look at me. You need to dial this back." He stroked Tyler's flushed cheeks with his thumbs. "Drew, I think it's best if you leave now. Go ahead to the casita and I'll come see you when I can." Cass never turned around, never let his focus wander from what his lover needed. He simply dismissed everything and everyone who wasn't Tyler Hardin.

You could spend a week searching every corner of your soul for answers...yet the most important lessons only took a moment.

*

Drew pulled his duffle from his truck and stood for a long minute staring at the two casitas. If he went to the left, he could be in the house he'd been promised once the renovations were complete. Even if it wasn't quite finished, there would be room for him and it would give him a fresh start. On the right was the home he'd shared with Holden. Never as a lover, never as a partner, but shared, nonetheless.

Now he was at an unanticipated crossroads. He'd stupidly assumed the world waited for him to get his shit together. He hitched his bag onto his shoulder and went inside.

Hours later, a knock at the door startled him from a restless sleep. He mumbled an invitation to come in, even as he pushed himself into a more comfortable upright position from where he'd crashed on the couch.

"Drew?" Cass called.

"Yeah, in here," he said, switching on the lamp. "Can I get you something to drink? Coffee? Beer?"

"No. I can't stay long. I need to get back to Ty."

"I really fucked up, didn't I?"

Without answering, Cass crossed the room and took a seat on the chair opposite the couch. Leaning forward, elbows propped on his knees, he gnawed on his lip before answering. Finally, he blew out a long breath. "Yeah, I suppose you did." There was a long pause, then he continued. "The thing is, Drew, you weren't the only one. You and me...well, we've never had to hide who we are. But the truth is, the world just isn't like that for everyone. It doesn't do a damned bit of good to get angry with people for doing what they need to do in order to survive.

"I had a hard damn time with Ty's past. I might not always like the choices he made or some of the things he had to live with, but all of those experiences made him who he is and they are all a part of him, part of his past. I love him and I plan to stay in his future. Do you understand what I'm saying?"

Drew nodded, but the acid burning a hole in his stomach churned to a new level of heat.

"After you left, Holden told us a bit about how he was raised. Drew, he wasn't in the closet. Not like we thought, not like Ty. It sounds as if he and his wife were happy enough. The stayed married nearly ten years and they had a son. I think if she hadn't killed herself, maybe they'd still be married."

"He was married? She killed herself?"

"It's still not what you think. There were a lot of family things at play. There still are because his mother is threatening to fight for custody of Alex, to take him away."

"Why are you telling me this? Where's Holden?"

"He had to go, Drew. It wasn't about you. In the end he had to protect his son."

"I thought..." It was like being tossed from a cliff in slow motion. He saw each of his hopes and dreams pass by on his way to land flattened on the ground below. It hadn't been what he'd believed at all. The love he'd imagined, the hopes that he could free this man from his fears...

"Drew...Drew!" Cass was calling his name, only it seemed like it was from a long way off.

Slowly he brought his gaze to meet the sympathy in Cass's eyes. "Do you know where he is?"

Cass looked at him for a long steady moment. "Yes."

Drew nodded. "Did he ask you not to tell me? Never mind. I can see the answer on your face. I think...I think I'd like to be alone, now."

****

"All right, Cass. I've finalized the report on Chad Ollom for you," Holden said. He stepped into the office area of the small apartment. The two-room apartment wasn't exactly his style, but there weren't many places for rent in Kingman unless you signed a twelve-month lease. He wasn't willing to commit that far ahead until after he was finished with the three-times-a-week physical therapy appointments.

"We can get to business in a minute," Cass drawled in his deep voice. "How are you doing, Holden? How's Alex settling in?"

"We're both doing okay. I'm going to try to find him a summer camp as soon as I'm cleared to drive. We're enjoying spending time together after being apart so long, but I know he needs to be with other people, too. And even though it's hot, he needs to get outside and run. Of course, now that the doctor switched me to using a cane I'm able to move around a lot better."

"No ill-effects from your little adventure with Ty?"

"None." He laughed a little, but it wasn't a happy sound. "Unless you count getting my head out of my ass. And thanks by the way. Rick just notified me that my mother has dropped her case for custody of Alex." He swallowed hard. "I believe I would have won if we'd gone to court, but I couldn't have afforded someone like Rick Bell under any circumstances."

"Rick's a good guy, and as a gay man with two kids, he's been through this on the personal front, so he's only too happy to help." There was a long pause, then both men spoke at the same time.

"Have you heard from…"

"Drew got back yesterday…"

Holden cleared his throat. "Sorry. Didn't mean to drag that up. That must mean we need to get back to business. About Chad Ollom…" He ignored the screaming desire to ask more questions about Drew.

He would have to be content with the knowledge that the man he loved was at the Willow Springs.

"All right. What did you find out?"

"Chad is exactly who he says is, and a little bit more. He's from the Arizona strip, estranged from his family, who are heavily involved in a fringe religion. He was homeschooled and has no juvenile record. There isn't any other information about his childhood available. Graduated top of his class from Northern Arizona University, degree in Elementary Education, and went on to finish his Master's. He applied for teaching jobs around Flag, but the teacher's college at NAU makes permanent positions hard to come by. He was a substitute teacher and worked construction to make ends meet." Holden took a sip of coffee while he scanned the rest of the report on his monitor.

"His bad luck came when he worked at a small private school on the northeast side of the state. They were considering hiring him for a permanent position when one of the parents found out he'd been active in the GLBT student group. She started a whisper campaign against him, saying he was a pedophile. If Rick had been his attorney, he might have come out okay in the end, but it was pretty insidious. Can't really prove you're not, know what I mean?"

"This is really important to me and the plans for the ranch, Holden. Are you sure?"

"I am as sure as I can be that there isn't a hint of anything hinky about Chad. Every one of the school administrators I spoke with gave him glowing recommendations. They all insisted they'd seen nothing to indicate any inappropriate behavior. They only got shifty about using him again because of the rumors. The kid's fucked for finding a job anywhere in northern Arizona because there are just too damn many other teachers already here. No school wants to be bothered to take a chance."

"Are you sure enough to leave Alex alone with him?"

"Without hesitation."

"Okay, then why don't you?" Cass asked.

"Why don't I what?" Holden had the distinct impression that the rancher was two steps ahead of him. Again.

"Why don't you and Alex come back to the ranch to live, Holden. Chad's going to run the camps that Ty wants to hold here. I've spoken to Chad, he's willing and interested in continuing to teach. Arizona law is pretty liberal about homeschooling, given our wide open territories."

Whatever it was he'd been expecting, it wasn't an invitation to come back. He and Cass had worked out an arrangement that would allow him to work from home…wherever home ended up once his therapy was finished and he could drive. Because of the lack of schooling in the remote part of the county, living permanently at the ranch had never been on his radar. His heart started to pound uncomfortably in his chest as he thought of what that might mean for him and Drew. Would Drew take him back? Could they make their relationship work?

When Cass cleared his throat, Holden realized he'd been lost in his thoughts for quite a while.

"Think about it, my friend. It doesn't have to end like this. Now I'll let you go. You come out here anytime. There will always be a casita waiting for you and Alex. With or without Drew."

Chapter Fourteen

"Are we there, yet?" Alex asked as they bumped along the graded dirt road to the WSR.

Holden didn't know if he wanted to laugh at the clichéd question or ask it himself. It had been three weeks since Cass had helped him find the temporary digs in Kingman. Now they were headed back to the ranch for the big July Fourth barbeque. The trip was the first long distance drive he'd made since the doctor had cleared him earlier in the week. As long as he promised to keep up with his exercise on his own, he was released from physical therapy and was finally free to begin making plans for a more permanent home for his son. Yet he hadn't been able to take the step of calling a realtor. Not in any of the cities he'd been considering. It was the first week of July, and school started in six weeks. Even if it was only kindergarten, having Alex enrolled in school with a stable home was important. He wanted to prove to himself and anyone else who might have cause to question, that he was a responsible parent.

He'd be lying if he didn't at least acknowledge part of the hesitation came because of the offer Cass made of a permanent home here on the ranch. Not just a temporary home that belonged to someone else, but real land, with a deed and a home built the way he wanted. The security screening business continued to grow and he could live rent-free in one of the casitas until his own place was ready. There was really only one thing holding him back.

As if reading his mind, Alex spoke again, excitement ringing in his young voice. "Do you think Drew will be there today? He promised I could ride Candy when she got all better. And hows come you don't want to live with him anymore?"

Swallowing hard at the unintended nature of the question, Holden thought about how to answer. Was his son really ready to hear his dad like boys better than girls? How young was too young? Finally, he settled on the truth.

"I like Drew very much, but maybe in a way that some of your friend's dads and moms like each other."

"I know. Grandma told me. She said you were a pervert and Ty and Cass were an a-bom-in-a-tion."

Reining in his temper, Holden pulled his truck to the side of the road and put it in park so he could turn and look at his son. "Alex, those words…"

"I know what they mean, Drew told me. Grandma used them before, that's how I remembered. She wouldn't let me play at my friend Soledad's house anymore when she found out there were two moms instead of a dad."

Tears hovered on his son's lashes and Holden wanted to curse his mother soundly for being a narrow-minded bigot and for hurting Alex. Instead, he unbuckled their seatbelts and pulled him onto his lap. "I'm sorry your grandma hurt you that way, Tiger. I believe she's wrong. People love who they love and it isn't anyone else's business. Your friend Soledad is lucky if she has two moms who love her."

Alex pressed his face against Holden's chest. "Daddy, is it my fault Drew left?"

"No, son. There is nothing...*nothing* at all that you did wrong. Sometimes, even people who love each other can find ways to mess things up. What happened between Drew and me was my fault, not yours."

"So why don't you say you're sorry?"

Blinking back the sudden sting in his own eyes, Holden kissed the top of Alex's head. If only life was that simple.

"Come on, back in your seat. Let's go see what Ty and Cass have planned."

*

"Alex," Ty called as soon as they got out of the truck. "You got here just in time. Cass and I are taking a few kids to the fishing pond. Come on, you can ride with me."

"Can I, Dad?"

Holden smiled at Ty. "No adventures." With an excited yell, Alex ran over to hang on Ty.

Laughing, Ty tipped his hat. "Nope, Cass will keep me in line." With an easy smile, he swung Alex up into his arms and the two of them trotted to join some of the others.

"Damn right I will," Cass said. He walked over and handed Holden an icy bottle of beer. "You are cleared to drink alcohol now, right?"

"Yes, boss."

"Boss, is it? Well, good. I hope you listened to me and brought a bag to stay overnight because it's going to be too late to drive back. You can have your casita. Of course, you might want to check it out while we take young Alex fishing. Might be something in there you need to straighten out."

Holden met Cass's steady gaze. "Drew's here? Did he know I'd be here?"

"Why the hell do you think he's staying inside out of the way? This ain't fucking high school, Holden. You want something, go get it. Now we'll be back in a couple of hours. Don't worry about Alex."

Holden looked to where his son was already playing with some children from the neighboring ranches. Ty and Chad seemed to have gotten caught up in a game of tag that involved freezing like a statue until someone on your team rescued you. Even as he watched, Alex released Ty, who promptly scooped the boy up, and the two of them went racing away, laughing like crazy. It was good to see.

He looked back at Cass and received an encouraging nod. "There are all kinds of families, Holden."

Suddenly, he knew there was nowhere else he wanted to be, except inside that casita, and in Drew's face. It was about damn time they talked. Without another word, he turned and started across the yard, ignoring the soft chuckle from the man behind him. He only paused a moment to tap lightly on the door, then stepped inside, closed, and locked the door behind him.

Drew sat in the living room, facing the television, his back to the door. "Go away, Tyler. I told you I don't want to go. And lock the damned door on your way out, I'm tired of people just dropping in."

"It's locked."

Drew dropped his head forward and twisted the remote in his hands. Neither man spoke, but finally, Drew pressed a button, and the set faded to black. Slowly he turned his head, still not coming around fully to meet Holden's gaze. "They should have told me you wanted your place back."

"Why?"

"So I could move my stuff next door—get out of your way."

"Look at me, Drew." When Drew turned to face him, Holden swallowed hard to keep from cursing. The hazel eyes were hidden in shadow, but not enough to hide the dark circles. "You look as if you haven't been sleeping."

"Well you look good. Lost the crutches I see. I'm really sorry about your place. You go back out to the barbeque and I'll clear out." Drew twisted back around and lifted the remote again.

Biting off a curse, Holden crossed to stand in front of Drew. Letting his cane fall to the floor, he reached for Drew's biceps and lifted until Drew was standing. Pressed nearly chest-to-chest, Holden released his grip on Drew's arms and cupped his face. He traced his thumbs over the lightly tanned skin, the rasp of beard rough against his palms. He pulled Drew forward until their foreheads touched. "We have two things we have to do this afternoon." His voice came out with that hungry growl that Drew brought out in him.

"We do?" Drew's whisper brushed over him and seemed to grab at his balls.

"We have to go into that bedroom and work out some of this tension that seems to have built up between us…"

"What's the other thing, because I don't think…"

"No, sometimes you don't think. And sometimes I don't think. That's why the second thing we have to do is even more important than the first. We need to start planning our forever, because if we're going to raise Alex together, we can't afford these kinds of misunderstandings."

Leaning back to search Drew's face for any clue to his thoughts, he saw the exact moment his words penetrated.

"Raise Alex? Together?"

"I love you, Drew. Raising a child might be a lot more commitment than you ever expected, but Alex and me are a package deal. I understand if you need time to think about it or if you don't—"

"Quit talking, Holden. Just give me a minute, okay?"

Warily, Holden released Drew and took half a step back.

Drew sidestepped and put another couple of feet between them. "I can't think when you touch me. I need to think."

Holden watched helplessly as Drew crossed to the kitchen to take a beer from the refrigerator. Without turning, he popped the top, his throat working as he swallowed the icy brew. Holden's stomach felt like the time he'd raced down the stairs and missed the bottom step. A sudden drop just before he landed too hard and off balance. What had he been thinking just blurting it out like that? Of course Drew would have questions. He might not be interested in being with a man who was a father, let alone having a son himself. He'd been caught up in thinking about making the ranch a home, but he knew he didn't want to make the decision without Drew, if they were going to be partners. He'd forgotten the most important part of that equation. The part where Drew agreed.

Bending to retrieve his cane, Holden moved heavily toward the door. "I'm sorry, Drew. That wasn't fair. You don't need to go anywhere. Alex and I are heading back after dinner. I'd like a chance to explain sometime." Then his hand was on the door and there was nothing else to do but leave.

****

"Holden, wait."

Holden left his hand on the knob, but rested his forehead against the door.

Drew's heart was hammering so hard in his chest he thought Holden might be able to hear it across the room. "Jesus, we're really bad at this," he said. He blew out a breath and swiped his hand through his hair.

"Bad at what?" Holden asked.

"The talking it out part. You want to explain to me, I want to explain to you... Can we...can we just sit for a minute. Part of me just wants to go with the first item on your list and go to bed." He grinned when Holden turned his head and met his level gaze.

"Let's just hold that thought for a minute, okay? We don't have to talk everything out first, but I do need to tell you how damn sorry I am." He held up a hand when Holden started to speak. "No, really. Please? Just a minute.

"From the moment I saw you I knew I wanted to be with you. And being an out and proud gay man, I assumed the only reason you didn't want to be with me was because you were in the closet. I wanted to fix you...free you from your fears." He rolled his eyes and Holden laughed, even as he moved back into the room.

"So, I owe you an apology for that." He took a step back as Holden started to move closer. He couldn't let Holden touch him, not yet, or he wouldn't be able to say what needed to be said. "I know a little bit about...your wife. I'm sorry, Holden. Really sorry."

Nodding, Holden said, "Karen was my friend. We made a beautiful son together, but we wouldn't have stayed together much longer."

"Because you realized you were gay?"

"No, because we didn't love each other. That's why it wouldn't have lasted. One of us was bound to find someone and fall in love eventually. Do you need a label so badly, Drew? Because if that's what it takes, I'll call myself gay. I don't care. I meant what I said…I love you."

Hearing the words again, stated so calmly, so matter-of-factly undid him. "Holden, you're talking about raising Alex together. This isn't just fucking around."

"No, it isn't. And I wouldn't ask if I wasn't sure. Drew, I'm not going to apologize for not telling you about Alex at first. I wasn't looking for a relationship." He paused and his lips twitched in amusement. "Gay or otherwise. Once we took that trip to Tucson, I knew I wanted to try to build something with you, but there were so many things in my life I needed to deal with. Honestly, Drew, I planned to tell you about Alex, but my mother was here when we got back and then everything went to hell."

"I know. And that's what I can't forgive myself for. Because your whole damn life was crashing and burning, and instead of digging in and asking what I could do to help…I ran away with my feelings hurt."

"That's not how I see it, Drew, but if you need my forgiveness, you already have it. Now, do you think maybe I could hold you?"

"If we do this...if we live together and raise Alex...will your mother—"

"No." Holden bit out an answer, cutting Drew's question in half. Then he softened. "Cass has an amazing attorney, who does a lot of work in these types of cases. He put together all the legal precedents, presented it to my mother's attorney, and convinced her to withdraw the case, at least for now. And if she decides to try again, she won't be able to prove I'm an unfit parent. Trust me, Drew, that's not a factor. What about you, though? I've never asked if you're interested in having kids."

Swallowing hard, Drew moved, finally closing the distance between them. Holden surrounded him in his strong arms, just folded him up close. "Yes, Holden. I never thought it would be possible...yes. Yes. Yes." He pressed a kiss to Holden's neck, breathing deeply of the scent of his soap mixed with sweat. "Yes." He kissed Holden's nose. "Yes."

"Come on, Yes man, let's go to bed."

*

Drew wondered if he'd ever be loved by this man enough that he wouldn't remember every time as though it was a first. Not this time. He'd always remember this as their first time as partners, as part of a forever that didn't only exist in Drew's mind. Holden had said the words, had asked him to share his son. Their son. He would remember this moment for the rest of his life. Especially since they'd come so close to losing it all. He would remember this kiss. The way Holden's big hands held Drew's face, the way his breath felt in the brief hesitation before their lips met. Remember the way he tasted as he swept into Drew's mouth. Holden kissed him with the promise of now, sweetened by the flavor of forever. He would remember the gentle preparation, his slow slide to ready under his lover's mouth and fingers.

In the dim afternoon light of the shaded room, Drew watched Holden's face as his lover pushed into him. A flash of white teeth against the warm darkness. Exotic, enticing, hot. Then everything slow and gentle was gone, washed away in a desperate need pounding though him like a wave. The urgency passed between them until they were dancing on the line of pain and pleasure. The stretch and burn momentary distractions before his legs were up and over Holden's shoulders as his cock drove so hard, so deep that every pulse of pleasure came with an equivalent twinge of pain.

Drew wanted to take him deeper, to pull Holden even further inside, to put himself between Holden and the rest of the world…to keep him safe from all the things that could hurt him. This wasn't the slow, easy lovemaking of two people confident they had all the time in the world. They came together with a violent certainty of two survivors, people who knew they'd nearly lost each other and would never willingly travel that hell again.

Holden moved inside him as if they were joined by liquid fire, melting into each other, until there wasn't a part of Drew that Holden didn't fill. Tongue in his mouth, fingers digging into his hips, heavy balls slapping against Drew's ass. Every stroke was like heat lightening, no storm, just a flash of electricity that burned bright, pulled at his nerves, scorched his skin. Then the heat spilled over, as Drew was flooded with warmth in his ass, on his belly, through his veins.

No, they hadn't just made love...they'd declared war on anyone or anything that got in their way.

****

"Ready?" Drew asked.

"Ain't the fucking prom, Drew," Holden said and wondered what it was about all these emotions that kept everything feeling on the edge of high school.

"Yeah, I get that. And you aren't in the closet. I get that, too. So why am I so fucking nervous?"

"Maybe because there's something you forgot to tell me?" Drew didn't think he was imagining the sulky edge to Holden's voice. He definitely wasn't imagining the frown line between Holden's brows.

"Was there? Must not have been important. I'll probably think of it later. Come on, I think I see Ty." Keeping his face carefully blank, Drew pushed past Holden to step out into the bright afternoon sunlight. The smoky smell of mesquite and grilling meat filled the air. Drew followed the progress of the four-wheelers as they slowly rolled toward the back of the ranch house with their precious cargo of kids all laughing and shouting from the pull-behind wagons.

"Looks like the party shifted to the back. That's a good thing, because it's much cooler back there." He grabbed Holden's hand and pulled him around the side of the house to the covered patio. He knew he was annoying his lover, and really, he didn't want to drag this out too long, but there was something he needed to do.

"Drew!" Alex's voice rose above the general chatter as the wagons unloaded and kids raced to tell their families about the fishing trip. He swore, seeing that miniature version of Holden running to him, arms outstretched, broad grin stretching his mouth wide. Well…there was just nothing…*nothing* to compare to what that sight did to his heart. Scooping the boy up, he twisted him around in a fierce hug, and knew he would die before he let anything happen to Holden's son.

"Alex, my man," he said. "Did you have fun fishing?"

"Yep. It's so cool here. They have their own fishing pond and everything. Ty made us put them all back today because he said there was already too much to barbeque." While Alex was talking, Drew carried the boy on his hip until they were in a shady spot of grass, between an orange and lemon tree, both heavy with fruit. He felt the weight of Ty's gaze, but he kept his focus on the story Alex was spinning. He was also aware that Holden had followed, but was hanging back slightly, presumably watching the two of them talk.

When the boy wound down, Drew stood him on the ground then squatted down so they were together at eye level. "So you like it out here on the ranch, Alex?"

"I love it. If Daddy and I come back here would you live with us?" The simplicity of the question tugged straight at his heart and sucked the air right out of his lungs. Swallowing against the urge to throw himself at the feet of the two Titus men, Drew tossed out a question he hoped would make young Alex laugh.

"That depends. Do you snore? 'Cause really, I can't sleep very well if you're going to make a lot of racket."

Alex dissolved into giggles. "Daddy sometimes snores. He sounds like a grizzly bear." The bear in question growled deep in his chest and swooped down to tickle his son before joining Drew on the ground.

Drew smiled at Alex. "Well, I suppose I can put up with a little noise...but I want to ask you something serious, is that okay?"

Alex glanced over at his father, then turned back to Drew, nodding with a solemn looking expression that Drew wanted to tease away.

"Do you remember when your grandma was here?"

"Yes." Alex's usually sunny face closed off and a small frown hovered on his mouth. He looked down and pressed his lips together as if to keep from saying something.

Drew glanced up at Holden, but didn't wait for him to intervene. Instead, Drew leaned forward and lowered his head until he was face-to-face with the young boy. "Hey, Alex. You can tell us what you're thinking."

"I didn't like it. She called Daddy a pervert."

Resisting the urge to either curse or close his eyes, Drew blew out a calming breath. "I'm sorry she said that, Alex. But that's kind of what I want to talk with you about. If I move here with you and your dad, other people might say the same thing or even worse."

"Daddy says you love who you love. He says it's okay that my friend Soledad has two mommies and that Ty and Cass are a family." Alex's dark eyes shone, and he looked over at his father. Holden smiled down at his son with such pride and love on his face that Drew was momentarily speechless.

Drew took Holden's hand in his, palm to palm, and threaded their fingers together. Reaching for Alex, he added his small hand on top of Holden's, then placed his other hand on top of the boy's, so that he held the Titus men sandwiched between his own hands. The worry that Holden wouldn't want him, didn't need him, melted away.

"Your daddy is right, Alex. You love who you love. Is it okay with you that I love your daddy, too? Can there be room enough in your family for me?"

With a whoop, Alex pulled their hands apart and launched himself at Drew, knocking him sideways into Holden. Big, strong arms surrounded him and pulled him until he was pressed back against Holden's chest, locked in place, while Alex scrambled to climb on top of the two of them.

"Does this mean we get to live here, forever, Daddy?"

"What do you say, Drew? Will you build a home with us and stay forever?"

"Yes! Oh...yes." Before he could say more, Holden cupped his jaw in his big hand and tilted Drew's head to capture his mouth in a kiss. For one breathless moment, everything stopped. Sight, sound, movement. Then, as if from a long way off he became dimly aware of cheers from the patio and the delighted squeals of the youngest member of his new family. Together, the three of them would make a home. He pulled back and met the dark gaze of the man who had come to be so important in his life.

"I didn't forget, after all," he teased. "I love you, too, Holden."

~~The End~~

Meet the Author

Laura likes it hot, which helps explain why she ended up Arizona after living in such diverse places as Japan, New Orleans, Maine, and Florida. She once enjoyed hobbies such as gardening and travel. Now the characters in her head compel her to tell their stories to her readers, so she writes. She shares her home with her husband and youngest son, two dogs, and a cat. Laura also writes under the name L.E. Harner, and her books can be found at Amazon, Barnes and Noble, All Romance eBooks, and other online retailers.

Connect with Laura at:

Twitter: http://twitter.com/lauraharner

Facebook: http://facebook.com/lauraharner

Or even better…check out the website at http://lauraharner.com

Also Available:

Forbidden Love

Detective Danielle Delacroiux is one kick-ass detective with the Généreux PD, and she's got a murder on her hands. By all accounts, Crease Martin was nothing but a homeless drunk and a lousy informant, but Dani counted him as one of hers. Now she'll stop at nothing to find his murderer. With a red silk handkerchief under the body as her first clue, Dani wants a quick break. When a handsome stranger practically strolls up to the crime scene, Dani can't help but notice his expensive Italian suit, red silk tie, and empty breast pocket. Could he be who she's looking for?

Dani is less than impressed when Mr. tall, dark, and yummy is introduced as the newest lawyer in town, and even worse, he's another of the Charbonnet offspring. The deadly feud between the Delacroiux and Charbonnet families goes way back, and there is one thing she knows without a doubt. If Hawk Charbonnet committed this crime, she'll be damned if his connections will do him any good. She'll happily lock his arrogant ass in jail for the rest of his life. Which would be a shame, because she had to admit, it was a fine-looking ass.

~*~

Part of Me

Jason's life hasn't been easy. Feeling responsible for the death of his twin the night they graduated from high school, Jason commits emotional suicide by revealing he's gay after his brother's funeral, permanently severing all ties with his ultra-conservative parents. But when he runs to Hunter Dane for comfort, all he can see is the same rejection mirrored on his best friend's face.

Twelve years later, Jason needs all the support he can get to beat back the cancer invading his body. When Hunter unexpectedly shows up to shift from former friend to caregiver, Jason must battle his attraction even while he's waging the biggest fight of his life.

~*~

Altered States, free prologue for the Altered States Series

New Orleans Police Detective Sam Garrett can't believe his bad luck when he's assigned to investigate a string of gay-bashings turned deadly in the French Quarter. Especially when he realizes Travis Boudreaux, his new, hot, and most-likely-straight partner, plans to use him as bait. The worst part? They've got no back-up because the rest of the city is preoccupied by another series of killings — the victims drained of blood.

~*~

Deep Blues Goodbye, Book One of the Altered States Series

The world might not have been ready for vampires when NOPD Detective Travis Boudreaux had the bad taste to sit up at his own funeral, but two years later, the new cause célèbre is civil rights for preternatural beings and most humans are on the bandwagon. Except whoever is killing vampires and wannabes.

Detective Sam Garrett hates all things preternatural. Having your undead partner try to make you his first meal will do that to a guy. One final screw-up gets Sam banished to the Paranormal Criminal Investigations Unit—the Odd Squad—under the oversight of Detective Danny Burkette.

Now it's up to Burkette to work with Garrett by day and Boudreaux by night as they follow a trail of clues that leads from the historic cemeteries of New Orleans to the bayous of southern Louisiana. Under the all-too-interested gaze of a Master vampire and the local werewolf pack Alpha, they discover some lessons in life—and death—take longer to learn…and not all second chances are created equal.

Warning: In this series the vampires don't sparkle, werewolves kill, and sometimes the men have sex. With each other.

~*~

Ty Hard, Book One of the Willow Springs Ranch Series

Tyler has used Don't Ask, Don't Tell as a shield against the truth since he was seventeen. Now, Ty finds himself cut loose from his Navy career after months of rehab from a debilitating head injury. At a loss as to what to do with his life, he travels to Willow Springs Ranch in Arizona to visit his surrogate father, only to arrive minutes after his oldest friend's death. Ty must come to terms with the loss while he fights to keep the PTSD from pulling him under. The last thing he's ready to think about is his growing attraction for another man.

Rancher Cass Cartwright's relationships never last more than a few hours, and that's just the way he likes it. Now he's in danger of doing the one thing he swore never to do: fall in love. Can Cass convince Ty to let go of his past or will sabotage at the ranch kill their love before it has a chance to grow?

~*~

Hold Tight, Book Two of the Willow Spring Ranch Series

Sheriff Holden Titus had organized his fresh start down to the last detail. Except for the part about the bomb that blew his plans all to hell. Now he's running out of time, without a job, without a home, and struggling to get back on his feet. Literally.

Despite the impolite rejection, Drew knows he didn't have the wrong impression months ago when he asked the sheriff to dance, but he never expected to have Holden's life in his hands. Literally.

Thanks to some meddlesome matchmaking, the two men are now temporary housemates at the Willow Springs Ranch and Drew is determined to help Holden heal, both physically and emotionally. Even if it means he has to drag the other man kicking and screaming to physical therapy...and out of the closet. In fact, that might be kind of fun.

The problem is, Holden doesn't consider himself in the closet...but not all secrets are created equal.

~*~

Oceans Apart, Book Two of the Separate Ways Series

It's been two years since Lord Jamie Mainwaring and Detective Remy Remington worked and loved their way through their one and only case before going their separate ways.

Now Jamie is once again mixing agency business with pleasure as he and his partner, Agent Ryan Whiteside, are assigned to a case involving piracy in the Caribbean.

Remy and his old friend Miggy are still detectives, but they've gone private in Phoenix. When their biggest client sends them to supervise an unusual diamond transfer, they think their toughest challenge will be maintaining their cover as a gay couple on a barefoot-style cruise.

When murder connects the dots between the two cases, the four men must learn to work together as relationships and loyalties are tested amid misunderstandings and memories on the high seas.

~*~

Rescued, Book, Two of the Three's Allowed Series

Elizabeth Ashford runs into the wilderness near a highway rest area, trying to escape her abusive husband before he kills her. Self-made millionaire and expert in high tech security, Michael Enwright is at the first rest stop of his long overdue sabbatical when he sees the fleeing woman and intervenes, saving Elizabeth's life, while nearly losing his own. When Michael's help is misinterpreted, he ends up handcuffed and face down in the dirt before Elizabeth can set her former lover, Sheriff Graeme Kennedy, straight. In order to protect Lizzie, Graeme is forced to work with Michael and brings both of them to his cabin for protection.

Now Graeme finally has Elizabeth under his roof, right where he's always wanted her. So why is he jacking off to visions of the drop dead gorgeous and take-charge Michael? Some things never change.